# THE PURE AND THE IMPURE

*also by Colette*

---

# Colette

---

# THE PURE AND
# THE IMPURE

TRANSLATED FROM THE FRENCH BY
*Herma Briffault*

INTRODUCTION BY
*Janet Flanner*

SECKER AND WARBURG

LONDON

First published in England 1968 by
Martin Secker & Warburg Ltd
14 Carlisle Street, London, w1

Copyright © 1966, 1967 by Farrar, Straus & Giroux, Inc.
Published in French under the title *Ces plaisirs* in 1932
and under the title *Le pur et l'impur* in 1941

Portions of this book previously appeared in
*Earthly Paradise*: Colette's autobiography drawn from
the writings of her lifetime by Robert Phelps

SBN: 436 10517 9

Set in 12 on 14 pt. Linotype Granjon
and printed in Great Britain by
Western Printing Services Ltd, Bristol

OF THIS CURIOUS VOLUME, *The Pure and the Impure*, in several ways unlike any other that Colette wrote, she eventually said, "It will perhaps be recognised one day as my best book." Its genesis probably sprang from diverse events and a new influence which rose in the year 1925 when she and Maurice Goudeket first met in the South of France, she approaching her fifty-third year, he just turned thirty-five, the digits for their respective ages being the same but reversed like mirror writing. Of her three husbands, only he, the last and the friendly favourite, served her literary genius with the devotion of a young neophyte. Her first husband, Henri Gauthier-Villars, considerably her senior and a Paris journalist of sorts, had stolen her opening four *Claudine* books, the first one published on the edge of the century in 1900, by publishing them under his professional pseudonym of "Willy". Indeed, it was not till a quarter of a century later, in 1926, that she finally established her literary rights to them by producing the original manuscripts, which she had saved, scribbled in durable notebooks such as French children used at school.

By 1925 she was divorced from her second husband, the handsome, worldly Henri de Jouvenel, editor of *Le Matin*, who had pointedly asked her why she could not write novels that were not immoral. In 1923 he had started the serial publication in *Le Matin* of her latest work, *The Ripening Seed* (*Le Blé en herbe*), now considered a classic of adolescent love, which *Le Matin* readers found so shocking that he had to stop printing it, unfinished. From it came her famous melancholy phrase, "Ces plaisirs qu'on nomme, à la légère, physique"—"These pleasures which are lightly called physical," meaning that they can also shake the soul. The first two words, "Ces plaisirs", formed the original title of this book you are now reading, which during World War II she inexplicably altered in a small, privately published de luxe edition to *Le pur et l'impur*. As *Ces plaisirs*, and before its publication in book form, it began to appear serially at the end of 1930 in a Paris weekly called *Gringoire*, whose editor, after the fourth instalment, discovered (just like Jouvenel) that his readers neither appreciated it nor liked it, and cut it off so short that the word *Fin*, The End, appears in the middle of a sentence that is never completed. Under either title, *Ces plaisirs* or *Le pur et l'impur*, this book has long been out of print except as part of the several definitive complete editions of Colette's works. It is a book that has led a life of its own.

When Colette met Goudeket, she was still at the high tide of her first fame. With the publication in 1920 of *Chéri*, her sensuously perfect, short tragic novel, at the age of forty-seven she had become one of the masters of French prose. She had also become a literary expert in verbal candour in her written portraits of female nudes,

[6]

which on canvas had been one of the loose glories of French Impressionist pictorial art. In earlier books such as *The Vagabond* and *The Innocent Libertine*, and in certain pages of the last *Claudine*, she had wielded an inspired pen as an intimate writer about women, with special interpretations. From Goudeket she received the strength both of euphoria and of renewed creative energy. By this time the posthumous volumes of Marcel Proust's *Remembrance of Things Past*—she had known Proust during World War I at his dinner parties at the Ritz— were appearing in Paris and his grand design as a writer had emerged, with its new specific sexual subject matter and its new masculine shape of love. Colette's favourite writing formula consisted of autobiographic novelizing. (In another two or three years she would write *Sido*, the chef-d'œuvre in this manner, her all-embracing biography of her mother, and of herself in her countrified child-hood.) But in her many short works and in her short stories she had already made use of most of her early life, except a certain portion of her middle-thirties, and its recollections. She now turned to these, without haste and at first not even boldly.

In 1928 a private Paris press published her character sketch of the Sapphic poetess Renée Vivien, born Pauline Tarn, in London, of an English father and an American mother, a fragile neurotic figure who spent most of her short, self-destructive life in Paris, maintained in mysteri-ous semi-Oriental elegance and living on spiced foods and alcohol in a garden apartment by chance next to Colette's, near the Bois de Boulogne. Colette doubtless chose her to write about first, in these pure and impure recollections of extraordinary women, because Renée Vivien was dead—had died two decades earlier, in 1909. This provided for Colette the long, useful, writer's retrospective so easily enriched by the passage of time as it began to shorten itself onto paper and to take its shadows from a pen dipped in ink. Renée Vivien's poetry, which included impassioned propaganda for the Mytilene myth, was symbolistic in style and touched by Mallarmé, as was natural to the period, but was carefully constructed and poetically valid, for her gift was genuine.

When she presented an occasional book of her poems to Colette, it was discreetly concealed in a basket of exotic fruits or flowers or wrapped in a length of Oriental silk. None of Colette's circle ever saw Renée's lover, or learned who she was, but she must have been very rich. She would send her carriage and coachman to Renée's apartment when Renée was giving a ladies' champagne dinner party, with an imperious command, always instantly obeyed, for Renée to leave her guests and come at once. The poetess repeatedly said she feared she would be killed by her, if only by a surfeit of love. Colette's study of Renée, which glows with brilliant writing and a certain pity, became the most vivid phantasmagoric portrait in *The Pure and the Impure* when it was finally published in Paris in 1932.

With its various contents assembled, its descriptions of the little bars and restaurants favoured by these special women in smoking jackets and long trousers, "worn like guilty pleasures", as Colette wrote, after describing herself in "a pleated shirt, stiff collar, sometimes a waistcoat", and always a manly "silk pocket handkerchief", it became clear, at least on second reading, if not on the first, that Colette in this new book had written a serious analysis of sex, of the sexual response and of sexual variety and ambiguity.

The book opens with an extensive appreciation of a woman Colette called "Charlotte", a generous cocotte who simulated long, nightingale-like cries of satisfied love because they gave felicity and a triumph of manhood to her dying lover. It was Colette's desire to add to the limited treasury of truthful insights into love, into the mysteries of love in its many forms. And in the new book she used her customary semi-fictional formula to report on the behaviour, the *mores*, reflexes, instincts of women, especially as sentient, desiring creatures drawn to similarities and even to substitutes. Colette, as author, confronts the reader at the same time in a somewhat fierce intimacy, with her personal remembrances, observations, and exact images, all dealing basically with the phenomenon of eroticism. Colette's understanding of the male sex amounted to an amazing identification with man per se, to which was added her own uterine comprehension of women, more objective than feminine. One can think of no other female writer endowed with this double comprehension whereby she understood and accepted the naturalness of sex wherever found or however fragmented and reapportioned. She seemed to have a hermaphroditic duality in her understanding and twofold loyalties.

One of the female figures in this transvestite society of the "Pure and the Impure" was a woman whom Colette called "La Chevalière", since her real title was too weighty to be mentioned, a quiet person, "with the solid build of a man, reserved and rather timid". Stripped of all the fictitious trappings with which Colette loyally sought to disguise her, she was easily recognizable to Parisians as the ex-Marquise de Belboeuf, with whom Colette had lived for six years after the end of her first marriage. To earn her living, Colette had become a music-hall dancer and mime, playing in Paris at the famous Ba-Ta-Clan and touring the provinces in an act called "Desire, Love, and the Chimera", in which she was costumed like a cat, with a feline mask and whiskers and a velvet tail. At certain times when funds were low, her travelling companion, the ex-marquise, had played a minor male dance role in the troupe. The father of the marquise was the Duc de Morny, illegitimate son of Queen Hortense of Holland, who was the daughter of Josephine Beauharnais by her first marriage—the famed Josephine who afterward became Napoleon's empress. Morny was thus a bastard half brother, on the distaff side, of Napolean III of the Second Empire. Morny married a Princess Troubetskoy, and they had three children, of whom the only girl was the Princess Marie, affectionately called by her governess the "Little Miss", which became "Missy" and her nickname for life. She had married the Marquis de Belboeuf, whose estates were outside Rouen. A French woman writer who as a child had known Colette and Missy at Colette's seaside home at Rozven, on the Brittany coast, still recalls Missy's astonishing appearance. She had fine features, her mother having been beautiful and her father handsome. She wore no make-up. Her face was oval, her teeth were pretty, and she had a very pretty nose. She looked like a distinguished, refined, no-longer-young man, for she always wore men's clothes, indeed wore quite a lot of them, which made her look plump. To hide what might have seemed her effeminate figure, she wore an assortment of woollen waistcoats and shirts, and because her feet were aristocratic and small, always wore several pairs of socks, so they would fill up her men's shoes. She was addressed as Monsieur le Marquis. In Paris in later life she lived in the Passy quarter, always as a man. At the funeral of one of her brothers, she attended in a mourning veil and a démodé black dress. She "looked like a man dressed as a woman", the younger members of the family said with disapproval, and they begged her to hasten back home and put on her male attire, which she refused to do, feeling somehow that it would be disrespectful to the dead.

At the bottom of the social scale in Colette's reminiscences in *The Pure and the Impure* came "Amalia X", a majestic, down-at-the-heels old actress she had earlier met in her theatrical career, still optimistically telling her own fortune with a pack of soiled tarot cards on a little café table and remembering aloud what her life had been. Of all Colette's offerings, this was the most realistic and the least pure, being comic, coarse, and basic in its simple sexual wisdom about women and their women who simulated to be men—basic on fundamental psychologies such as only the poor can afford to understand, with their indifference to convention and their patience on matters which in their experience ranked merely as kinds of odd love. Amalia, who had travelled, had lived as one of the Western women in the palace of a pasha in Constantinople, from which she would go out at night, and at some risk, to keep her rendezvous with some little French blonde. "I had everything," she affirmed to Colette, "beauty, happiness, misery, men, and women ... You can call it a life!" she concluded and went on turning over the tarot cards to discover what could not happen tomorrow.

At almost the end of her book, Colette astonishingly turned antiquarian. She cited the long lives of two well-born English ladies who in the spring of 1778 (just after the founding of the United States of America and just before the French Revolution, neither of which interested them) had run away together to live in reciprocal happiness and poverty for fifty-three years in Llangollen, a small town in Wales. The elder of the two, Lady Eleanor Butler, had kept their diary of continuous small joys, referring to Sarah Ponsonby, her companion, in substantive terms such as "my Love", or "my Delight": "Read Mme de Sévigné. My Love drawing:" Or: "At ten my Beloved and I drank a dish of tea. A day of most delicious and exquisite retirement." Or: "Sweet sunshine, blue sky, birds innumerable. My Beloved and I went a delicious walk round Edward Evans' field." Sir Walter Scott and other distinguished travellers finally began calling on them, for the grace of their elegant manners and concentrated tenderness. There is finally, in *The Pure and the Impure*, also a report on jealousy between women in which Colette remarks that "in an eternal triangle there is always one person who is betrayed, and often two."

[12]

And thus ends this curious concentrated volume which Colette herself said should one day be regarded as her best book. It would be heretical to argue. What one most misses in it is her voluptuous writing about nature, with which she was so impetuously and watchfully in love, writing which is necessarily absent here—descriptions of fleshy fruit buds and sharp green new leaves, of willow sprouts as yellow as hair, of colours and odours in spring or autumn hedgerows. All of this praise of animate speech-less vegetal nature in fields and forests has perforce been omitted from this book whose concern is human passion and physical sexual love, which are customarily practised indoors.

How long Colette has lived, even after her death!

*January 1967*                                    JANET FLANNER

THE PURE AND THE IMPURE

# ONE

THE DOOR THAT OPENED TO ME on the top floor of a
new building gave access to a big, glass-roofed studio, as
vast as a covered market. Half-way up the high wall ran
a wide balcony draped with Chinese embroideries, the
rather slapdash kind manufactured in China for the
export trade, the designs large but rather pretty all the
same. A grand piano, some flat little Japanese mattresses,
a gramophone, and potted azaleas accounted for the rest.
With no surprise, I shook hands with an acquaintance,
like me a novelist and journalist, and I exchanged nods
with my unknown hosts, who, thank God, seemed to be
as little inclined as I was for any friendlier exchange.
Quite expecting to be bored, I settled down on the mat
allotted to me and watched the opium smoke wastefully
and sluggishly streaming upward to collide, as if regret-
fully, with the glass panes of the skylight. Its black, ap-
petizing aroma of fresh truffles or burnt cocoa bestowed
upon me patience, optimism, and a vague hunger. I decided I liked the dull red glow of the shaded lights, the
almond-shaped white flames of the opium lamps, one of
them near by, the other two flickering like will-o'-the-
wisps farther on, in a kind of alcove under the balustraded

balcony. Someone leaned over that balustrade, a youthful head caught the red ray of the hanging lanterns, a loose white sleeve wavered and disappeared before I could make out whether the white silk sleeve and the head of hair slicked down like the hair of a drowned person belonged to a woman or a man.

"You're here as a sightseer?" my writer friend inquired.

He was stretched out on his little mattress, and I noticed he had exchanged his dinner jacket for an embroidered kimono and was displaying the affected ease of the opium smoker. My one desire was to escape him, as I do with the French people, always a nuisance, that I meet abroad.

"No," I answered. "On a professional assignment."

He smiled.

"I thought as much. Writing a novel?"

And I loathed him still more for thinking me incapable —as indeed I was—of enjoying this luxury, this tranquil if rather base pleasure, a pleasure prompted only by a certain kind of snobbishness, a spirit of bravado, a curiosity more affected than real . . . I had brought with me only a well-concealed grief which gave me no rest and a frightful passivity of the senses.

One of the unknown guests came to life, rose from his couch to offer me a pipe of opium, a pinch of cocaine, or a cocktail. At each refusal he raised his hand limply in a gesture of disappointment. He finally handed me a box of cigarettes, and with an English smile said, "Really, can't I do anything for you?"

[18]

I thanked him, and he took care not to insist.

After more than fifteen years, I still remember that he was handsome and apparently sane, except that his eyes were too wide open between the rigid eyelids people have who suffer from chronic insomnia.

A young woman, intoxicated as far as I could judge, noticed my presence and announced from a distance that she intended to come over and give me "a dirty look". She repeated it several times: "Yes, exactly, a dirty look." I don't recall any other cheerful incident to report. A few serious smokers, only half visible in the reddish gloom, made her shut up. I believe one of them gave her some opium pellets to chew, an act she performed dutifully, making a faint sucking sound, an animal sound like an infant at its mother's breast.

The opium, which I do not smoke, permeated this ordinary room with its fragrance, and I was not at all bored. Two young men with their arms around each other aroused the attention of my fellow journalist, but they made no disturbance, merely talking rapidly in low voices. One of them continually sniffed and wiped his eyes with his sleeve. The red gloom in which we were bathed could have lulled the strongest minds. I was in an opium den, but not in one of those assemblies which give the spectator a rather lasting disgust for what he sees and for his own participation by being there. I rejoiced at this and hoped that no naked dancer of either sex would come to disturb our devotions, that there was not the least danger of an invasion of alcohol-soaked Americans, and I even hoped the gramophone would fall silent . . .

Just then a woman's voice was raised in song, a furry, sweet, yet husky voice that had the qualities of a hard and thick-skinned velvety peach. We were all so charmed that we took care not to applaud or even to murmur our praise.

"Is that you, Charlotte?" asked one of my prone and motionless neighbours after a time.

"Why, of course it's me."

"Sing some more Charlotte . . ."

"No!" angrily shouted a man's voice. "She didn't come here to sing!"

In the distant red gloom could be heard the indistinct husky laughter of "Charlotte" and the whispering of the same irritated young man.

Towards two o'clock in the morning, while a sleepless young fellow was serving us cups of very fragrant pale Chinese tea that had the scent of new-mown hay, a woman and two men entered, bringing into the odorous and murky air of the studio the cold night air caught by their furs. One of the newcomers asked if "Charlotte" was there. A teacup crashed at the far end of the room, and again the young man's angry voice was heard.

"Yes, she's here. She's with me, and it's nobody's business. You can just leave her alone."

The new arrival who had asked the question shrugged, threw off his overcoat and dinner jacket as if preparing for a scuffle, but merely put on a black kimono, then quickly sank down beside one of the opium trays and began to smoke a pipe, inhaling with such disagreeable avidity that one felt like offering him sandwiches, cold roast veal, red wine, hard-boiled eggs, any food no matter what, more suited to appeasing his ravenous appetite. The woman in furs who accompanied him went over to the drunken girl, whom she called "My sweet", and I had no time to condemn their friendship for they went to sleep at once, moulded together, the hips of the one in the lap of the other, like two spoons in a silver-drawer.

In spite of the stuffy warmth of the room, cold air came down from the skylight, announcing the night's ending. I wrapped my coat tightly about me, deploring the laziness, induced by the heavy aroma, which, combined with the late hour, still kept me from going home to bed. I could have followed the example of the sensible people lying there, could have stretched out with them and slept without fear, but although I can confidently sleep on a terrace or a bed of pine needles, any shut-in and unfamiliar place makes me uneasy.

The narrow staircase of polished wood creaked under some footsteps, which then sounded on the balcony above me, where could be heard the rustling of silk, the light impact of pillows thrown upon the echoing floorboards, and silence closed in again. But from the depths of this very silence a sound imperceptibly began in a woman's throat, at first husky, then clear, asserting its firmness and amplitude as it was repeated, becoming clear and full like the notes the nightingale repeats and accumulates until they pour out in a flood of arpeggios. . . . Up there on the balcony a woman was trying hard to delay her pleasure and in doing so was hurrying it towards its climax and destruction, in a rhythm at first so calm and harmonious, so marked that I involuntarily beat time with my head, for its cadence was as perfect as its melody.

My unknown neighbour half sat up and muttered to himself, "That's Charlotte."

Neither one of the two sleeping women woke up; nor did the snuffling young men, indistinctly visible, laugh aloud or applaud the voice that broke on a subdued sob. On the balcony above, the sighing left off. And the quiet ones down below all felt the chill of the winter dawn. I hugged my furred coat about me, and a man lying near by pulled up a corner of embroidered cloth over his shoulder and shut his eyes. At the far end of the room, near a silken lantern, the two sleeping women drew still closer to each other without waking up, and the small flames of the oil lamps flickered under the down draft of cold air from the skylight.

Stiff and aching from my prolonged immobility, I stood up and surveyed the prostrate forms on the mattresses, mentally calculating how many I would have to step over on my way out. At that moment the balcony stairs creaked again. A woman in a dark coat had come down and was on her way to the door. She stopped before reaching it, buttoned her gloves, carefully pulled her veil down to her chin, opened her handbag, jingled some keys.

"I'm always afraid . . ." she murmured.

She was talking to herself, but when she saw that I was going out, she smiled at me.

"You're leaving, too, Madame? Then follow me, if you want to have light in the stairs—I know where the time switch is."

[22]

In the staircase, where her hand brought forth an un-flattering light, I could see her more distinctly. She was neither tall nor short, was rather plump and resembled the favourite models of Renoir—the same full face and short nose, recalling the belles of 1875, and this so strongly that in spite of her smart olive-green coat with fox collar and the small hat currently fashionable, she somehow looked out of date. Probably forty-five years old, she still had a youthful freshness, and her eyes that looked up at me in the curves of the stairway were large and gentle and grey, grey-green like her coat.

It was still dark outside, and the cool night air revived me. The desire that is a daily occurrence with me on clear mornings to escape towards fields and forests, or at least towards the nearby Bois de Boulogne, made me hesitate when we reached the pavement.

"You don't have a car?" said my companion. "Neither do I. But at this hour there are always cars to be had in this neighbourhood."

As she spoke a taxi appeared, coming from the Bois. It slowed down and stopped. She stood aside.

"Do take it, madame," she said.

"Why, not at all! Let me invite you . . ."

"Not to be thought of! Or allow me to take you home . . ."

She checked herself, making a gesture of excuse that I easily understood and protested.

"You're not being at all indiscreet," I said. "I live not far away, on the outer boulevard . . ."

We got in. The taxi turned around. The faint light of

[23]

the meter now lit up, from time to time, the face of the woman, who was unknown to me except for her first name, true or false, "Charlotte".

She stifled a yawn, and sighed.

"I'm not yet myself, and I live away out near the Lion de Belfort . . . And I'm exhausted . . ."

In spite of myself I must have smiled, for she looked at me without embarrassment and spoke with charming simplicity.

"Oh yes, I know, you're laughing at me, I can see what you're thinking."

What seduction was in her voice, how delightful the way it rasped out certain syllables and the suave and defeated way it had of letting the ends of phrases fall into the lower register . . . The window was open at the right of Charlotte and the breeze wafted towards me her rather ordinary perfume along with a brisk natural odour of healthy flesh, pleasant except for the smell of stale tobacco.

"It's really too bad," she began, as if at random. "That poor boy . . ."

"What poor boy?" I asked, submissively.

"You didn't see him? No, you couldn't have seen him . . . But you had arrived when he leaned over the balustrade of the balcony. He's the one in the white kimono."

"And fair-haired?"

"That's right," she exclaimed softly. "That describes him. He worries me a great deal," she added.

I permitted myself that smile of arch understanding that so ill becomes me.

"And merely worries you?"

[24]

She shrugged.

"Believe what you like."

"That young man was the one who made you stop singing, wasn't he?"

"Yes. It makes him jealous. Not that I have a fine voice, but I sing well."

"I was on the point of saying just the contrary, believe it or not. You have a voice . . ."

Again she shrugged.

"As you like. Some people say one thing, some say another. Shall I have the taxi stop just short of your door?"

I grasped the arm she had raised.

"By no means. Please."

She appeared to be a little upset over her uncalled-for discretion and made shift to ask a question that disguised a confidential piece of information.

"It isn't very harmful, is it, for a young man with weak lungs to take a little opium from time to time?"

"No, not too harmful . . ." I answered doubtfully.

A heavy sigh lifted her high and rounded bosom a little higher.

"He's a great worry," she repeated. "But don't you agree that when he's been good for a fortnight, taken his pills, eaten his red meat, slept as he should with his windows wide open, he deserves a recompense now and then?"

She laughed softly, a husky but musical laughter.

"He calls that an orgy, just imagine. He's proud . . . Oh, madame," she exclaimed, "the dustmen are at your door. Do you mind their seeing you arrive? No? How nice! Freedom is a wonderful thing. But as for me . . . I'm not free."

She fell silent, absently held out her hand, and gave me the faint little innocent smile of her large eyes, clouded with green like the pools the sea leaves at ebb tide.

# TWO

I DID NOT SEE CHARLOTTE AGAIN for some time. Nor
did I look for her, at least not in the places where I
imagined I might find her, for example, a church wedding on the Left Bank, or having tea in an ancient apartment, in the bosom of those families that rigidly preserve
their provincial ways in Paris. I imagined that her presence
at a small hexagonal table crowned with sweet biscuits
would have seemed quite natural to me. Seated in her
olive-green coat, her small hat tilted over her eyes, the
short veil raised like a slatted blind on her nose, the cup
of insipid tea held in two fingers, I saw her, I invented
her, I heard her accent of modesty and truth skilfully con-
vincing the cross-grained old hostesses: "As for me, you
know, the way I see it . . ."

I did not look for her, because I was afraid of dispelling
the mystery we attach to people whom we know only
casually. But I was not surprised to find her standing in
front of me one day when I was selling books for the
benefit of some charity or other. She bought a volume,
smiling at me in the most discreet way. I asked her, with
an eagerness that seemed to astound her: "Shall I dedicate
the book, madame?"

"Oh, yes, madame ... If it isn't asking too much."

"Not at all, madame ... To what name?"

"Why, simply put 'To Madame Charlotte ...' "

To all this repetition of "madame" that we ceremoniously exchanged, Charlotte added a chuckle that I
recognized, a subdued laughter, as gentle and poignant
as the language of the little nocturnal barn owl, that ring-
dove of darkness ...

And I put a maladroit question.

"You're all alone?"

"I never go out except alone," replied Charlotte. "We
haven't seen you again there..." She spoke in a half
whisper, leafing through the volume she had just pur-
chased. "*They* are always there on Sunday evenings..."

I accepted this indirect invitation for the pleasure of
seeing Charlotte again. The pleasure turned out to be
greater than expected, for I found her alone in the studio
opium den, which was as accessible and inhospitable as a
railway station. No irritable young man watched over her
in the depths of the red shadows amassed under the balcony. Bare-headed, very neat, and looking rather plump
in her black dress, she had not donned the ritual kimono.
She was drinking maté and offered me some in a
hollowed-out black and yellow gourd that had the
mingled odour of tea and flowering meadows.

"You can use this bombilla, I've just scalded it," she
said, handing me the spatulate reed tube. "Are you comfortable? Want a cushion at your back? Just see how quiet
we are tonight. None of those women ... You ask who
are those men at the far end of the room? English-

men, very proper people who come here only to smoke opium."

Her tranquil kindness, her muffled voice, and the expression in her grey-green eyes would have opened the hardest heart. Her plump arms, the eloquent and lady-like dexterity of her every gesture—what snares for the young and irascible lover!

"I see you're alone, Madame Charlotte?"

She assented with a nod, serenely.

"I'm taking a rest," she said simply. "You'll say that I could rest at home. But one doesn't rest well at home."

She let her assured and kindly gaze wander, and inhaled deeply the odour of the opium, which I myself was enjoying as only those who do not smoke can enjoy it.

"Whose place is this?" I asked.

"To tell the truth, I don't know," said Charlotte. "I first heard about this place from some painters. Do you really want to know?"

"Not really."

"As a matter of fact, your question surprised me . . . It's so pleasant not to know where one is . . ."

She smiled at me confidingly. To put her still more at ease, I could have wished that she did not know my name.

"Your young friend isn't ill, I hope?"

"No, thank goodness. He's with his parents, in the country. I expect him back in a week."

Her face darkened a little, and her eyes gazed into the reddish, smoke-filled gloom of the studio.

"How tiresome," she sighed, "how tiresome a man can be that one loves! I don't much enjoy telling lies."

[29]

"What do you mean? Why should you tell lies? Don't you love him?"

"Of course I love him."

"Well, then . . ."

She turned upon me a magnificent stare of contempt, at once mitigated by what she then said, politely.

"Suppose we say I don't know anything about it."

But I recalled the romantic reward she had granted the young lover, the almost public display of pleasure she had made in that nightingale lament, those full notes reiterated again and again, precipitated until their trembling equilibrium broke in a climax of torrential sobbing . . . No doubt this held Charlotte's secret prevarication, a melodious and merciful lie. I considered the young lover's happiness was great when measured by the perfect dupery of the woman who thus subtly contrived to give a weak and sensitive boy the very highest concept of himself that a man can have . . .

This substantial Charlotte was a female genius, indulging in tender subterfuge, consideration, and self-denial. And here she was, this woman who knew how to reassure men, sitting beside me, limbs relaxed, idly waiting to take up again the duty of the one who loves best: the daily imposture, the deferential lie, the passionately maintained dupery, the unrecognized feat of valour that expects no reward . . . Our concealed identity and accidental proximity, the surrounding atmosphere of so-called debauchery were alone what had loosened the tongue of this heroine whose silence in no way embarrassed me, this stranger to whom I told nothing, as though I had finished telling her all I had to tell . . . Her presence lured other ephemera from the depths of my memory, phantoms I seem always to be losing and finding again, restless ghosts unrecovered from wounds sustained in the past when they crashed headlong or sidelong against that barrier reef, mysterious and incomprehensible, the human body . . . They recognized Charlotte, for they had, like her, not talked except in safety, that is, to strangers, in the presence of strangers. A conspiratorial ear, quite often mine, had been within reach, and they had dropped into it their name, to begin with—an assumed name, but freely assumed—then, pell-mell, everything that burdened them: the flesh, always the flesh, the mysteries and betrayals and frustrations and surprises of the flesh. It was always a low, rapid, monotonous whispering, issuing from an invisible mouth smelling of wine, of fever, of opium—or else the sedate tone of a naked lady, pretentiously dignified—or the bitter revindications of one of those women who think men owe them something, and whom Hélène Picard would call a "Madame How-many-times"—all these confidences containing some seeds of truth, bobbing about on the surface of a rich deposit of unfermented and unfiltered wine. And I reflected, "In a few minutes, just a few more minutes of agitated conversation, I shall learn from Charlotte what she hides from her shy young lover."

In this I was mistaken. I should have recognized in Charlotte a creature weary enough to sit down and rest on any milestone, but strong enough to start off again unaided . . . She smoked some cigarettes, poured water from a small kettle over some fresh maté, called out to

[31]

an invisible person asking what time it was, and gave me a few pieces of information that she considered useful.

"I myself bring the maté here," she said. "The electric kettle is mine. But 'they' will provide you with anything you want, sandwiches, tea, biscuits. In which case, you slip fifty francs to the concierge downstairs... Don't be upset, madame. The last time you came, you only drank a cup of tea and smoked one or two cigarettes, so you haven't much on your conscience... And I hope you'll not offend me by offering to pay me for that cup of maté. Good, isn't it? A light tonic and not enervating... For those who smoke opium, there's another arrangement: the five pipes my boy smokes every time he comes here, for instance, are charged to a separate account."

A regulation as clear as this in what must be called debauchery would no doubt have distressed anyone else, but I was pleased with everything in Charlotte. A woman past her prime has a dozen ways, all unacceptable, of designating "the little spouse", "the bad child", the "sweet sin", the "little girl"... Charlotte said "my boy", adding to her ambiguous maternity a forthright, authoritative, no-nonsense accent. I was hoping that she would not turn out to be a version of those nuns, those nuisances we run into at every turn. By "nuns" I mean those predestined women who sigh between the sheets, but with resignation, secretly enjoying abnegation, needle-work, housework, and sky-blue satin bedspreads, for lack of any other altar to adorn with the virginal colour... They take fanatical care of their man's clothing, especially of his trousers, that bifid and mysterious garment.

[32]

From this they sink into the worst perversion, which is to hope and pray for their man to fall ill so they can handle dirty basins and clammy rags... I assured myself that Charlotte's conduct was in another category of behaviour. Her comfortable indolence elevated her in my esteem: so few women know how, with empty hands, to remain motionless and serene. I observed her feet and hands, relaxed and drooping, revelatory signs of wisdom and self-control...

"How well you seem to know how to wait, Madame Charlotte!"

Her large roving eyes, the pupils dilated by the darkness, turned back towards me.

"Yes, that's so, quite well. But now, as retired doctors say, I no longer practise."

"One always waits. And you said just now, 'I expect him back in a week...'"

"Oh! Yes..."

She waved her hand as if waving to someone passing in the distance, then again turned towards me.

"It's true, I am waiting for him. But I expect nothing of him. There's a shade of difference... I wonder if you understand what I mean."

"I believe I do."

"It would be too wonderful, the love of such a young man, if only I didn't have to pretend..."

She sighed, laughed, her pleasant round face wearing an expression that Renoir would have cherished.

"Isn't it funny," she said, "that in such a couple it's the older one—he's only twenty-two—who happens to be

[33]

obliged to lie? I'm devoted to that boy, with all my heart. But what is the heart, madame? It's worth less than people think. It's quite accommodating, it accepts anything. You give it whatever you have, it's not very particular. But the body . . . Ha! That's something else again! It has a cultivated taste, as they say, it knows what it wants. A heart doesn't choose, and one always ends up by loving. I'm the living proof."

She slid down wearily on the quilted mattress and rested the back of her neck on a cold little cushion of white woven straw. Lying thus, she could follow the play of light and shade cast on the reddish ceiling by the flame of a small unused opium lamp, now joining, then disjoining two pale rings, fringed and faintly golden. As I did not reply, she again turned to look at me, without raising her head.

"I don't suppose you understand me . . ."

"But I quite understand you," I assured her promptly, adding with involuntary warmth, "Very likely, Madame Charlotte, I understand you better than anyone in the world."

The smiling look in her eyes was my recompense.

"That's far from trifling, what you've just said. How nice that we know each other so little! We can talk about things one doesn't talk about with friends. Friends, women friends, if such a thing exists, never dare to confess to each other what they really and truly lack . . ."

"Madame Charlotte, do you ever try to find the thing you 'really and truly' lack?"

She smiled, her head thrown back, showing in the con-

[34]

fused light the underside of her short, pretty nose, her rather full chin, the faultless arc of her teeth.

"I'm not that simple-minded, madame, nor that shameless. What I lack—I simply do without. No, no, don't praise me for it ... But when one knows something really well, having once possessed it, then one is never completely deprived. Perhaps that accounts for my boy's great jealousy. Try as I will—and you have heard me and know I'm not ungifted—my poor boy, who has intuition, flies into senseless rages and shakes me as if he were determined to break me to pieces ... It's laughable," she said. And in fact she laughed.

"And ... the thing you lack ... is it really beyond reach?"

"Probably not," she said haughtily. "But I'd be more ashamed of the truth than of the lie. Just imagine, madame ... if I were to let myself go like a fool and not even know what I was doing or saying ... Oh! I can't bear the idea!"

She must even have blushed, for her face seemed to darken. In agitation she turned her head from side to side on the white cushion, her lips parted, like a woman threatened by a paroxysm of pleasure. Two points of red light attached themselves to the back-and-forth movement of her big, glistening grey eyes, and it was not hard to imagine that, were she to stop lying, Charlotte merely risked becoming more beautiful ... I told her so, tactfully, and only succeeded in rendering her rather cool and circumspect, as she had been in the taxi. Gradually she controlled her emotions and shut herself off from me. With a

[35]

few words she barred me from the domain that she seemed so arrogantly to despise and which bears a red and visceral name: the heart. She also barred me from the cavern of odours, of colours, the secret refuge where surely frolicked a powerful arabesque of flesh, a cipher of limbs entwined, symbolic monogram of the Inexorable ... In that word Inexorable, I gather together the sheaf of powers to which we have been unable to give a better name than "the senses". The senses? Why not *the* sense? That would offend no one and would suffice. *The sense*, dominating the five inferior senses, for let them venture far from it and they will be called back with a jerk—like those delicate and stinging ribbons, part weed, part arm, delegated by a deep-sea creature to ...

O intractable, lordly senses, as intractable and ignorant as the princes of bygone days who learned only what was indispensable: to dissimulate, to hate, to command! Yet it is you that Charlotte held in check, couched beneath the quiet night soothed by opium, assigning arbitrary limits to your empire ... but is there anyone, not even excepting Charlotte, who can fix your unstable frontiers?

I flattered myself that Charlotte, who sought my approval, might also try to enlist my sympathy. But nothing of the sort happened. At the approach of dawn she punctiliously returned to banalities by way of two or three rather charming commonplaces, such as "The only really masterful sound a man makes in a house is when, on the entrance landing, he fumbles with his key in the lock of the door ..." When she stood up to go, I remained lying on my little mattress, pretending to sleep. She fastened her coat collar unhurriedly and carefully at her round throat, the refuge of that deceptive warbling, and the red sparks left her large eyes as she pulled down a fine veil over her face before going out.

How many shadows still conceal her ... It is not for me to dispel them. When I think of Charlotte, I embark upon a drifting souvenir of nights graced neither by sleep nor by certitude. The veiled face of a woman, refined, disillusioned, is a suitable preface to this book which will treat sadly of sensual pleasure.

# THREE

I NEVER HAD TO GO OUT OF MY WAY to be let in on masculine secrets. The average man overflows with confidential talk when he is with a woman whose frigidity or sophistication sets his mind at rest. And it strikes me that at a time of life when a woman will go on and on exulting, misty-eyed with enduring gratitude, over the riches that have slipped through her fingers, over the cruelty, the infamy, the arrogance of the donor, a man at the same age will nurse a rancour that time does not heal.

My friend X, a celebrity, never leaves off his good humour and natural reserve except when calling to mind, in intimate conversation with me, his past as a celebrated lover. "Oh, the bitches!" he exclaimed one evening. "I was never spared a single embrace by any of them." (He did not say "embrace", but used a blunter term that refers to the terrible paroxysm of male sexual satisfaction.)

Rarely have I encountered in a woman the kind of hostility with which a man regards the mistresses who have exploited him sexually. The woman, on the contrary, knows herself to be an almost inexhaustible store of plenty for the man ... Am I, then, going to find myself, in the first pages of a book, declaring that men are of less use to women than women are to men? We shall see.

But let me return to the famous lover I have just quoted. Like most men capable of servicing (if I may put it that way) a great many women, possession, which is lightning quick, provoked in him a wretched feeling of hopelessness —the neurasthenia of the Danaïds. If I understood him rightly, he could have wished to find at long last a woman who would love him enough to refuse herself to him. But it is hard for a woman to refuse herself. And besides, at the moment when our conqueror glimpsed the veritable purpose of love and the pure and burning space that unites, better than the bonds of flesh, two perfect lovers, he was seized by desire so strongly that he flung the object of his love to the floor and possessed her on the spot.

"Ah, what a life!" he sometimes sighed.

I have always greatly appreciated his confiding in me and I hope our confidential talks are not ended. As a rule, we choose for our rendezvous a quiet, private dining-room in a first-class restaurant in the centre of town, the building an ancient one with thick walls that do not vibrate. We dine like gourmands, after which my friend X paces up and down, smokes, and talks. Occasionally he raises the ball-fringed curtain and looks out. On the other side of the glass appears a strip of Paris, animated and silent, calling to mind a swarm of fireflies on a lake of asphalt, and I am enveloped in the facile illusion of danger lurking in the night outside, of safety within the old walls warm with secrets. That feeling of security increases as I listen to the man who is talking, for mine is the very human pleasure of witnessing catastrophes. I am fond of this man, who from time to time reveals himself to me, but I am also fond of seeing him denuded and stewing in his boiling cauldron; besides, he refrains from calling out for help.

With the passing years, he shows signs of the neurosis that dishonours the voluptuary: the obsession with statistics: "There's no arguing the fact," says he, "my average is lower. But after all, no one could care less than I do." And then he rages once more against "those little bitches that keep score on a man". I talk to him, then, about Don Juan and tell him I'm surprised that he has not yet written a Don Juan novel or play, and he gives me a compassionate look, shrugs, and charitably informs me that "period plays" are as out of fashion as cape-and-sword romances. And suddenly he exposes the child hidden in the heart of every professional writer, a child obstinately infatuated with technique, flaunting the tricks and wiles of his trade. His pretended cynicism marvellously rejuvenates him, and I let him run on.

Once I confessed to him that I was thinking of writing a play on the subject of Don Juan grown old, a part designed for the aging actor Édouard de Max.

"Don't do it, my dear," he urgently advised.

"Why not?"

"You aren't sufficiently Parisian. Your concept of Don Juan, my dear—why, I can just see it. What would it add to the other concepts of Don Juan? A pleasant acrimony, a great show of gravity on licentious subjects, and to end up with, you'd find some way or other of inserting a dash of rustic poetics... Don Juan is a hackneyed type, but no one has ever understood him at all. Fundamentally, Don Juan . . ."

At this point, of course, my famous colleague expounded his own concept of Don Juan, who, to hear him talk, was a serious-minded tempter, a kind of diplomat of annexation, who seduced a woman tactfully and was soon bored.

"Don Juan, believe me, my dear, was another one of those men who think only of taking, another one of those grasping men whose way of giving is no better than what they give. Of course, I'm speaking from the voluptuary's point of view."

"Of course."

"Why 'of course'?"

"Because when you talk about Don Juan you never talk about love. The business of numbers gets in your way. That's not your fault, but . . ."

He gave me a sharp look.

". . . but such is your tendency."

The hour was late and the cold of a streaming wet night seeped between the curtains, which were fastened together with a safety-pin. Otherwise, I would have talked to my friend about my own concept of Don Juan. But X was already gloomy at the thought of the next day, worrying about his work and his pleasures, especially the latter, because there comes a time in life when one feels on safer ground alone than when trying to find pleasures with another.

The rain had stopped when we parted, and I announced that I wanted to go home alone and on foot. My friend the seducer went off with the characteristic stride of a long-legged man, and looking very handsome, I thought. A Don Juan? If you like. If the ladies like . . . But this Don Juan is obsessed with his reputation and pays the price of his vanity with the punctuality of a timid debtor.

We saw each other again not long afterwards. He was looking tense, high-strung: his features can age in a quarter of an hour and be rejuvenated in five minutes. Youth and old age come to him from the same source: the eyes, the mouth, the body of a woman. In thirty-five years of orderly work and disorderly pleasures, he has never found time to be rejuvenated by rest. When he allows himself a vacation, he takes his poisons along with him.

"I'm going away," he said.

"That's good."

He glanced at his reflection mirrored in a shop window.

"You think I look tired? I am."

"Tired of whom?"

"Oh, all of them, the she-devils . . . Let's have some orangeade. Here, or farther on . . . wherever you like."

When we were seated, he put up his hand to smooth his silver-grey hair.

" 'The she-devils,' " I repeated. "How many are there, for goodness' sake?"

"Two. That sounds like nothing, two . . ."

He brazened it out, laughing and wrinkling his big, classic nose, the typical nose of a woman's man.

"Do I know them?"

"You know one of them, the one I call Ancient History. The other is new."

"Pretty?"

"Oh, indeed!" he exclaimed, tossing his head and rolling up his eyes so you could see only the whites. This facial exhibitionism is one of his traits that I dislike.

"She's a Tahitian kind of beauty," he went on. "At home, she goes about with her hair hanging loose down her back, hair as long as that, a mane of hair flowing down over that length of red silk she wraps around her body . . ."

His expression changed, he stopped rolling his eyes.

"It's all humbug, sham, a fiction, of course," he added savagely. "I'm not taken in. But she's quite sweet. I'm not dissatisfied with her. It's the other one . . ."

"She's jealous?"

He gave me a hesitant look.

"Jealous? Oh, that one is a real demon. Do you know what she's done? Have you any notion what she's done?"

"You're going to tell me."

"She's taken up with the new one, they're bosom friends. Ancient History talks about me to the new one. That disgusting way they have of telling each other everything! She describes our love-making, our 'amours' as she calls it, and of course burlesques it into an orgy. She recalls everything and makes up the rest. After which the Tahitian beauty . . ."

". . . expects to get as much out of you . . ."

He looked at me with a new and sad humility.

"Yes."

"My dear man, allow me to ask a question. With the

[43]

Tahitian girl, is it real sensuality or merely athletic prowess and a spirit of competition?"

My celebrated friend changed countenance. I had the pleasure of seeing a whole series of expressions appear on his features—defiance, cunning, every nuance of primordial hostility. He fixed his eyes upon the distant and invisible adversary and blew out his cheeks.

"Pooh!" he scoffed. "That's an old story, I can handle it. A question of dog eat dog. And as for her sensuality, I'm cultivating it. She's young, she's reckless, you know. It's rather amusing . . ."

He threw out his chest and was again a man of distinction.

"Anyway, the girl is, when excited and dishevelled, a marvellous sight. What splendour . . ."

There is a short scene in the play *Célimare le bien-aimé* where the lover, hurriedly shut into an adjoining room by his mistress as her husband appears, kicks and pounds the locked door. "What's that?" the husband asks. "Nothing . . . Some workmen are repairing the chimney next door," stammers the trembling wife. "But this is intolerable! Pitois," he says to the old diplomatic footman, "will you please go and tell those fellows to make a little less noise!" Pitois hesitates, then says, in embarrassment, "Sir, those fellows don't look very accommodating." "Oh yes?" says the husband. "So you've got cold feet? Well, then, I'll attend to it myself." He approaches the locked door and shouts with all his might: "A little less noise, you there! We can't hear ourselves think!" A horrified silence. "That's the way, Pitois," says the husband, "that's the way to talk to workmen. I can do it myself." Upon which Pitois goes out, after this aside: "I'm going. I really feel sorry for him."

I was mischievously recalling these lines of Pitois as I sat there facing my friend X, who was claiming victory over a silly girl, insatiable and reckless. I smiled to myself and changed, or at least appeared to change, the subject.

"I understand that you are preparing a warm reception for your colleague from the North?"

X brightened up, for he is by nature enthusiastic and for some time now has left behind him all professional jealousies.

"You mean Maasen? Yes, indeed. A great man! I intend to have a front-page piece on him in the *Journal*. There will be a banquet and speeches, all very high-flown and humbug. I would like to see the Académie mobilize the best it has for him. A great man, very great. And you'll see, his political career has just started. He has everything. He's one of those men I call 'the well-endowed'. He has an extraordinary animal magnetism, a handsome head, silver threads among the gold now, of course, but there's still a look of youth about him . . ."

"Yes, I know. I even know . . . They say that . . ."

"They say what? Affairs with women?"

"Naturally. They say . . . Lean over, I can't shout this sort of thing!"

I whispered a few words in my friend's ear. He replied with a long whistle.

"By Jove! But what documentation, my dear! Those *are* impressive figures. Who gave them to you?"

[45]

"On this kind of information, all sources are suspect."

"Well said."

He straightened up and buttoned his coat like an offended man about to challenge another to a duel. His brown-gold eyes held a wicked gleam.

"Oh, those Nordics!" he joked. "I'd just like to see them . . ."

Suddenly conscious of betraying ill humour, he tried to cover up.

"All the same, I don't see how this . . . ornamental detail can be of interest. When we are concerned with a man like Maasen, that magnificent human edifice," he added, with gross irritation, "I don't care whether or not the edifice includes a room with mirrors and the appurtenances of a brothel . . ."

"Of course," I said.

He paid for our two orangeades and picked up his gloves and stick.

"At any rate," I said, "you'll let me know, I hope."

"Let you know what?"

"Why, of Maasen's arrival. I'd like to talk to him."

"Oh! Yes. Quite. A rather keen little wind this, isn't it?"

"A wind from the North . . ."

He acknowledged this mediocre thrust, giving me a piercing look.

"Heavens," he said, "you think I'm a little more than jealous of Maasen, don't you! All the same, I've not yet sunk so low as to indulge in physical jealousies!"

I shook my head in denial and affectionately patted his

[46]

bristly six o'clock cheek. "My dear man," I felt like saying, "is there such a thing as non-physical jealousy?"

He went off, and it was to his swinging back, his exaggeratedly long stride, and to his hat that I addressed myself mentally. Especially the hat, the significant, informative, inconstant, perplexing hat! For a boyish look, he sets it too much on one side; for a bohemian look, it's tilted too far back; and when it's tilted too far forward, that means, "Watch out, we're sensitive and can be tough, let no one tread on our toes." In sum, a hat that refuses to grow old.

Thus once again X and I played at awaking the echoes of that fulgurant climax of possession, the paroxysm waggishly called *le plaisir* or, euphemistically, "satisfaction" —nomenclatures I must adopt, though unwillingly. We can talk about it, perhaps, because it has never threatened us together, never pinned one upon the other; or perhaps because my friend lets me see, in his fine "courtship plumage" which he so frequently dons, the bald spots and the clipped quills ... We have our habits. We begin by talking a little about our work, about the people passing by, about the dead, about yesterday and today, and we compete with each other in pleasant incompatibility: "No, the way I see it, not at all. On the contrary, I ..." "How strange, I hold a diametrically opposite opinion ..." It needs a word or a name and we fall again into our habitual pile of cinders, black for the most part, but glowing red here and there. Except for the fact that he is the one who talks and more often than not I am the one who listens, I feel as responsible as he, since, from the minute he first sets his feet in the ignited traces, I follow him and

[47]

even goad him on. Having gone beyond the limit one day, he expostulated.

"Too much has been said and too much written about this. I gag at all the literature that deals with the consummation of love, do you hear me, it makes me vomit!"

With my fist held in his fist, he pounded the table.

"It's time you did," I said. "You should have vomited on it before writing your share."

"And what about you?"

"Oh, that's something else again! I do myself this justice: I've always waited, before describing the conflagration, to be a little at a distance, cool and in a safe spot. Whereas you . . . In the very midst of suffering, in the very midst of joy, oh dear, it's indecent."

He nodded soberly in agreement, flattered.

"Yes, yes," he murmured. "What an aberration!"

He smiled as if he were twenty-five, with a feigned sadness and a feigned humility that were charming.

"I have behaved like those shipwrecked voyagers who pitch into the cargo and gorge themselves until they can eat no more. And they eat no more, for nothing is left, and what will they eat tomorrow?"

"Exactly, my dear man, exactly. But invariably something will be found when the need is felt—a barrel of anchovies at the bottom of the hold, or a case of dried beef, or a quantity of grapefruit and coconuts . . ."

He shrugs. He meditates. He talks. He talks about *it*. I learn how he overwhelms women with letters, telegrams, telephone calls. He laments, he waits at a spa, he hides on a Swiss mountaintop, he makes and endures innumerable scenes, emerging from it all steaming, as if from a hot bath, thinner and regenerated. There is nothing of Byronic gloom about him. Rather, he's a war horse, he rears and charges against what he does not comprehend. He is full of voices that are the echo of his own voice. He is too important for the women not to feel the need to imitate him, too masculine to elude the girl who puts on a show of being terribly naïve. The girl would never be able to fool you, Don Juan, my Don Juan as I see you!

When I had the daring idea of making known my "concept of Don Juan", Édouard de Max was still alive. He is dead now, and I no longer consider writing the play in which I wanted him to take the leading part.

"Édouard," I said to him, "how do you feel about it?"

"I'm too old, my dear."

"Exactly. But for my play I need to have you old."

"Then I'm not old enough for the part. You've hurt my feelings."

The expression in the blue-green-gold eyes and the sound of his voice cast a spell.

"But I also need to have you very seductive."

"Well, that I can still be, thank God. Youth is not the time to seduce, it is the time to be seduced. What does your Don Juan do in the play?"

"Nothing yet, the play isn't written. And not much when it is written. I mean to say, he doesn't make love— or at any rate, only a very little."

"Bravo! Is it indispensable to make love? Oh, it's all right to do it, but only with women to whom one feels indifferent."

[49]

I am quoting Max faithfully, for the pleasure of putting his words beside those of a great lover, Francis Carco, the novelist. Just listen now to Carco: "Ah," he sighs in moments of simplicity and gloom, "a man should never go to bed with a woman he loves, that spoils everything . . ." And I want further to quote Charles S.: "The difficult thing is not so much to obtain a woman's ultimate favours, but rather, once she has yielded to our desires, to prevent her from setting up housekeeping with us. What else can we do but run? Don Juan has shown us the way."

"Édouard," I went on, "you've got to understand me."

"I'm afraid I will," Max agreed, and his charming smile lost all its gaiety. "Haven't I already understood?"

I explained my famous project and repeated the name Don Juan twenty times. Without our being aware of it, the warmth and magic of that name wove a spell: Édouard's expression changed as, mentally, he assumed the role. I could see his lips compress, his deep-set eyes sparkle blue and gold, the colours of the water salamander; I was aware of his magnificent mane of hair trembling as he moved his shoulders, and could see his hand gradually reach for the hilt of a sword . . .

"You see, after the age of fifty, Don Juan . . ."

The interval of a dress rehearsal at the Théâtre Marigny shed an unflattering light on us and on the gardens, the acid, cold green of springtime. It was there, for the last time, that I promised Max that he should create the part of a misogynous Don Juan. "Make haste", he said to me. Alas, he was more prompt than I and descended for ever towards the wavering secondary characters with whom I had not yet had time to pair him off. I had already decided that around him, around Don Juan in his maturity, there should be as many women as possible, and for the most part young, and that he would detest them. For I counted on taking as my model a man known to me, and who no doubt is still more or less alive somewhere or other.

As for that man, it took me quite a while, some years ago, to see that he was Don Juan, because what little he had to say about women was offensive.

A persistent youthfulness clung to his features, without improving his looks, and indeed it was rather a curse. Besides, he had no need of it. I can't figure out whether women were drawn straight to his eyes, bathed in a false and saline mistiness like grey oysters, or to his lips, always shut over his small and regular teeth. All I can say is, they were drawn straight to him. Where he was concerned, they at once acquired the set purpose of somnambulists and bruised themselves against him as if against a piece of furniture, to such an extent did they seem not to see him. They were the ones who designated him to me by his true name, Don Juan. Without them, I would never have thought of applying that name, of humble origin really, born of a very few pages, but eternal, for no other name in any language has ever supplanted it.

One of his most striking characteristics was the fact that he never hurried. Golf, tennis, riding kept his diaphragm flat and his muscles in trim. But I confessed to him my surprise that, except for games, he was always last to arrive at functions where politeness or the obligation to be pleasant should have been his guide.

"It's not out of laziness," he replied very seriously, "but to maintain my dignity."

I laughed and all too readily agreed with his rivals, who sneered at the offhand attitude of this man who was more successful with women than they. "That imbecile, that idiot of a Damien . . ." I am here bestowing upon him a name which recalls his true name, a rather old-fashioned one . . .

Later on, while I was working on *Chéri*, I tried to persuade myself that Damien, young, could have served as model for me, but I soon saw that Damien, a stiff and rather limited sort, was far from having the indulgent whimsicality, the impudence and boyishness indispensable to Chéri. They had nothing in common except a similar melancholy, and a keen intuitiveness, extraordinary in Damien.

One day he showed me, in confidence and out of vainglory, the cabinet where he kept his letters from women. It was a tall piece of furniture, impressive beneath its bronze appliqués, and was provided with a hundred little drawers.

"Only a hundred!" I exclaimed.

"The drawers are subdivided inside," Damien replied, with the solemnity that never left him.

"And do women still write letters?"

"Yes, they write. A great many do, really a great many."

"Quite a few men have assured me that women nowadays merely use the telephone, reinforced by a few *petits bleus!*"

"The men to whom women don't write nowadays are simply men to whom women don't write, period."

I liked being with him, as I like being with swift animals who are motionless when at rest. He talked little, and I believe he was second-rate in everything except the performance of his mission on earth. When I finally overcame his mistrust, I was greatly edified by his sententious and quasi-meteorological manner. It was almost identical to that of country people who forecast the weather, understand the temper of animals and the intentions of the wind —I believe I need look no further for the secret of our apparently unjustifiable friendship.

To amuse and astonish me, he kept me informed as to how he "lured" women to their fall, one misstep after another. Please note that, unlike his ancestor, he did not seduce cloistered little ninnies, whining little Catholic pussycats, warm and weaned. It took little prowess, certainly, to seduce Inés!

I was dumbfounded, however, at the monotony and simplicity of the amorous manœuvres. Between Damien and the women there was not the slightest hint of diplomacy. It was rather a question of merely pronouncing the magic word, "Open sesame!"

I believe he concealed a rather modest family background. This would explain his agreeably exaggerated reserve, his discreet vocabulary. His successes were neither retarded nor reduced by this; on the contrary, since a great many women have a secret aversion to men of gentle

[53]

birth. At the risk of being thought older than he was, he did not use the current slang. When we established our friendship, Damien was becoming almost as hard on himhelf as on "them", his women. Old age, declining powers, and physical decrepitude were condemned by him according to the code of the primitives who kill off the aged and execute the infirm. Merciless—in a well-mannered way.

I put some questions that must have seemed rather naïve—for instance, the following exchange.

"What memory, Damien, do you believe you left with the women, with most of them?"

His grey eyes, which were usually half closed, now opened wide.

"What memory? Why, without a doubt, a feeling of not having had quite enough."

The tone of his reply shocked me, although it was too curt for me to notice at once its fatuity. I surveyed this cold man, who was not at all affected, whose good looks were not in the least banal or standardized. The only flaws I could find in his physique were his hands and feet, which were too small and dainty, a detail that I find important. As for his grey eyes and dark hair, that is a contrast that vividly strikes us women and we say, complacently, that it is a sign of a strong character.

The man of strong character deigned to add a few words:

"Whether I had them at once or let them languish a little, I had to leave them the minute I was sure they would blame me for ruining them. That about sums it up."

I know that every métier begets its particular lies and litanies, but even so, I listened to Damien incredulously. "I had to . . ." But why did he have to? I put the question.

He replied in his usual firm voice, his usual dry manner, as if he were predicting the bad weather to be expected at the next full moon, or a devastating scourge of caterpillars.

"You surely wouldn't expect me to dedicate myself to their happiness, once I was sure of them? Besides, if I had spent my time making love, I would never have been the Don Juan I was and am."

I recall that this instruction was imparted to me between midnight and two o'clock in the morning, in one of those unpredictable towns where darkness is the glacial opposite of daylight and where only the night makes one aware of the nearness and attraction of the sea. Damien and I were drinking a sweetish orangeade drowned with water, a hotel orangeade, an end-of-the-season orangeade, and were sitting beneath the glass roof of a hotel lobby.

Damien had come to my dressing-room to fetch me after my pantomime act. "I'm in this town rusticating," he had briefly explained, using a word that was out of date. He abstained from alcohol. "It brings grey hairs," he said, leaning over his goblet to show his dark hair, which was rather plentifully threaded with grey, glistening like aluminium. He sipped his orangeade thoughtfully through a straw, and as my eyes rested on his fine mouth, I reflected that there was something about it that aroused ideas of sweetness, of sleep, something secret and gentle and sad—and still youthful. And I remembered the adage: "A kissed mouth never grows old."

I have often thought about this man who had neither wit nor gaiety nor the disarming coarseness that women find delightful and reassuring. His only asset was his function. I have tried to persuade myself a hundred times that nothing in him stirred my senses, only to admit a hundred times that this was only a part of the truth, the plain and short, the meaningless part of the truth.

"You had to leave them," I repeated. "But why? Is victory all you want? Or, on the contrary, is this victory of no importance to you?"

He turned my question over in his mind. Then, as if it had reached him from a long way off, he clapped the palms of his hands together and forcefully interlaced his fingers. I expected him to let out a torrent of abuse, to speak out, to say no matter what. I wanted him to give way to anger, to make some kind of row that would prove him to be illogical, weak, and feminine—what every woman wants every man to be at least once in his life. I wanted to see him roll up his eyes pathetically, wanted him to show the ugly empty whites, instead of those eyelids like shutters, slanted down, cautious, sheltering the proud and reproving gaze of his lowered eyes. Nothing that I wanted to happen happened. Instead, Damien began to talk quietly, in short and abrupt phrases that I would be hard put to recall and write down, because the meaning of the words cannot be separated from their sound or from the monotonous delivery, with frequent pauses, which helped Damien at times to hide and at others to express the deepest resentment.

Not for a moment did he lose the least dignity, at any

[56]

rate the physical dignity of a man accustomed to live his life in public. He did not let out any of the crude old words that we all carry in our subconscious since our childhood, since our schooldays. He named no one and committed only one error of taste, the casual reference to his mistresses in mentioning the title or rank or social position of their husbands or protectors. "... She was the dear and close friend of a great industrialist ..." "Her husband was a peer of the realm ..." "Good God, you can't imagine how boring a Balkan grain dealer can be to a woman!"

He talked for a long time. My hotel darkened; in the late hours we were allowed only a reduced light which fell from the high ceiling. A night watchman in correct livery but wearing preposterous carpet slippers shuffled across the hall.

"Well now, please tell me," said Damien, "what did I get out of all this?"

Listening is an effort that ages the face, makes the neck muscles ache, and stiffens the eyelids looking fixedly at the speaker. It is a kind of studied debauch ... Not only the listening, but the interpreting ... the elevating to its secret meaning a litany of dull words, promoting acrimony to grief or wild desire.

"By what right? By what right did they always get more out of it than I did? If only I could doubt that they did! But I had only to look at them. Their satisfaction was all too real. Their tears, as well. But their satisfaction especially ..."

At this point he did not indulge in any digression on the bold immodesty of females. But imperceptibly he threw

[57]

out his chest, as if to shake off what in effect he was seeing in his mind, likewise "subdivided inside".

"They allow us to be their master in the sex act, but never their equal. That is what I cannot forgive them."

He took a deep breath, pleased at having so clearly rid himself of the essential motive of his long, low-voiced lament. He turned from one side to the other, as if to call a waiter, but all the night life of the hotel had withdrawn into a single human snore, nearby and regular. Damien therefore satisfied himself with the rest of the tepid soda water, composedly wiped his gentle mouth, and smiled sweetly at me from the depth of his wilderness. The night passed over him softly, and his vitality seemed to be a part of a particular asceticism ... At the beginning of his confidential talk he had successively singled out, to show them off better, the famous mistress of the great industrialist, the titled lady, the actress, but from then on he used only the plural. Lost among them, feeling his way through a crowd, through a flock, scarcely guided by such landmarks as a breast, a hip, the phosphorescent furrow of a tear ...

"Sensual pleasure, satisfaction, good, yes, satisfaction, that's understood. If anyone in the world knows what it is, I'm the one. But beyond that to ... No, really, they go too far."

He shook out what remained of his drink on the rug, like a wagoner in a country inn, and without excusing himself. Were those drops of warm water meant to insult a woman or the entire invisible horde that had no fear of the conjuration?

("They go too far." They go, to begin with, as far as the man leads them, and the man demands a great deal in his conceit, his intoxicating conviction that he is imparting an arcane science. Then, the very next day, he says, "What has become of my innocent girl of yesterday?" He sighs and exclaims, "What have I in common with this she-goat at a witches' revel?")

"Do they really go so far?"

"You can believe me," he said laconically. "And they keep going, they don't know how to stop."

He averted his eyes in a way that was characteristic, ostensibly, like a man who, confronting an open letter, refrains from reading it for fear of betraying on his features what he might thus dishonestly find out.

"Perhaps it was your fault. Did you never give a woman time to get used to you, to become mollified, to relax?"

"What in the world!" he scoffed. "Peace, after all that? Cucumber cold cream for the night and the newspapers in bed in the morning?"

He stretched himself discreetly, his only confession of nervous fatigue. I respected his silence, the elliptical word of a man who had never in his life treated with the enemy or laid aside his armour or admitted the least failure of energy—which is a kind of repose—to enter into his love-making.

"In short, Damien, you have the same concept of love that used to be characteristic of young girls, who could not imagine a warrior except with his weapon drawn or a lover except ready at any moment to prove his love?"

"There's something in that," he conceded, "and on

[59]

that score the women I've known never have had any reason to complain. I educated them well. But as for what they ever gave me in exchange . . ."

He stood up. I was afraid of recognizing in him another haggling trader, disappointed in a bargain—for I had met and known one elsewhere and at closer range. I was afraid of finding the answer to his riddle and of having Don Juan change before my eyes into merely an unlucky creditor. I therefore hurried to reply.

"What they've given you? Why, I should think, their grief. So you're not all that badly paid after all, are you?"

He showed me then that he was neither governed by his model nor jealous of him.

"Their grief," he repeated, "yes, their grief. That's very indefinable. And I don't appreciate it as much as you think. Their grief . . . I'm not a mean person. I only wish that I could have received—if only for a moment—as much as I gave."

He started to go. Again I held him back.

"Tell me, Damien . . . Aside from the men I've seen you speak to, have you any male friends?"

He smiled.

"Oh, really! *They* wouldn't have tolerated it."

Buried beneath that conglomeration of women, he had had no ventilating shaft to provide him with some fresh air . . . But just as I was about to regard the life of this man with horror, I suddenly thought that any alteration in the design, any "repentance" would have turned a modestly legendary figure into a pitiful caricature. Grotesque, the idea of a jovial Damien being consoled for his wicked women by pals who would slap him on the back and give him their advice: "Forget it. Come along, friendship is ..." I had just imagined this final downfall when Damien reassured me, with that severity which, for lack of other virtues, constituted his self-respect.

"I have nothing to say to men and never had. Judging from the little time I've spent with them, their usual conversation is sickening. Besides, they bore me. I believe," he hesitated, then concluded, "I believe I don't understand men."

"You exaggerate, Damien. It would have been different had you been obliged to earn a living and been put in daily contact with men, or if women had ruined you materially ..."

"Ruined? Why, please, ruined? What's money got to do with the topic we're discussing, which, by the way, has kept us up so late here—I really wonder why."

He was losing patience and checked himself.

"You've been told," he went on more gently, "that the idea of money inevitably enters into love affairs. You've been told ..." He smiled, in good fettle despite the late hour. "Too bad you don't have a son. I would have taught him the few words that a man like me should know ..."

I protested: "... and which would have doubtless been useless, for I simply cannot see myself with a son who would resemble you."

"Have no regrets," he said with disobliging sweetness. "Not everyone can have a son like me. I scarcely know

[61]

more than two or three such men, and they are quite circumspect. Even so, I will speak the few words to you, which you'll not understand: 'Give nothing—take nothing.'"

I was dumbfounded.

"You see," Damien noted gaily, "I'm delighted! I was always a little afraid you weren't any more intelligent than other women. Now, my dear, I must excuse myself for having stayed so long."

"Wait," I exclaimed, catching him by the sleeve. "If you want to keep your prestige with me, explain yourself. I don't always respect what I don't understand. 'Give nothing, take nothing.' What exactly do you mean by 'nothing'? Neither flowers nor jewels nor banknotes nor art objects? Are you thinking of *bibelots*, gold, credit, furnishing, real estate?"

He gravely inclined his well-shaped head.

"Exactly, all that. It is hard, I admit, not to break the rule. But one soon perceives that the bracelet is poisoned, the ring unfaithful, the card case or the necklace disturbers of dreams, the silver eager to land on the gambling table . . ."

It was fun to see him becoming sententious again, glorying in a science he had invented, and as positive as a village soothsayer.

"So one should neither give nor receive?" I laughed. "And if the lover is poor, his mistress indigent, then both she and he must tactfully let themselves and each other die?"

"Let them die," he repeated.

[62]

I had accompanied him as far as the revolving glass door of the lobby.

"Let them die," he said again. "It's less dangerous. I can swear on my word of honour that I never gave a present or made a loan or an exchange of anything except ... this ..."

He waved both hands in a complicated gesture which fleetingly indicated his chest, his mouth, his genitals, his thighs. Thanks no doubt to my fatigue, I was reminded of an animal standing on its hind legs and unwinding the invisible. Then he resumed his strictly human significance, opened the door, and easily mingled with the night outside, where the sea was already a little paler than the sky.

I treasure the memory of that man. Although I have never lacked close friends, rarer in my life have been the friends who were not close, between whom and me passed a sensual current, a mysterious force that made them, to begin with, rather cantankerous and sparkling, then dull, snuffed out like a candle. I enjoyed seeing Damien fixed in his error—as we call any faith that is not ours. Besides, he satisfied the liking I have always had for the mysterious void, and for certain privileged creatures and their steadiness in a supposedly paradoxical equilibrium, and especially for the diversity and steadfastness of their sensual code of honour. Not only honour, but poetic feeling, as when Damien applied his lyricism to abandoning his mistresses and letting them die. "Let them die," he said, and he said, "I *had* to leave them." He would have been baffled had

I told him (as I never did) that in his "I had to leave them" resided his simplicity, and that when he thought he was being coldly calculating, he was being a poet and a fatalist. His thankless and well-loved duties shut him off from everything else, and I could have learned a lot from him and about him had he not, in his hatred of any contest of wits, practised the empiricism of the wild beast teaching her young: "Look. This is the way I jump, this is the way you ought to jump." "Why?" "Because this is the way to jump."

I linger over this memory. If Damien is still alive, he is now more than seventy years old. Has the time come for his deliverance? And once freed, what does he amount to? If he reads these lines and this book, in which I hope to add my personal contribution to the sum total of our knowledge of the senses, he will smile and shrug, the tranquil little grey-haired gentleman. If in his latter years he has married some stouthearted woman, he will keep it quiet that he was Damien: this will be his last pleasure and his supreme deed of darkness. What could be the avowable end of Damien, other than a premature death? But there is no premature death for a man utterly dedicated to conquest, solitude, and vain flight: he is always at an age to die.

He embodied that type of man whom other men unanimously refer to as "a person devoid of all interest". When, by chance, he had to deal with ordinary men, he was always, I noticed, the one who was embarrassed and momentarily at a disadvantage. And if in his presence they told the usual off-colour jokes, he barely gave a sign that he heard. However, surrounding him there was an expanding zone as subtle as a perfume, gradually perceived by the men present, and with aversion. They justified this aversion as best they could. "What does that character over there do for a living?" one of them asked me, adding, "I can't stomach him. I'll bet he's a paederast." I could hardly keep from laughing over the suspicious man was betraying his own naïve and equivocal behaviour—he was limp with anxiety and as irritable as a prude on the point of letting herself be seduced, as he cast contemptuous glances at the suspected man, the very glances I had seen one of Damien's mistresses dart at him before she succumbed. She, too, had referred to him as "that character", to begin with. And when she stood up after sitting beside him, she brushed her skirt as if to shake off some crumbs. That gesture was, I felt, almost a morbid tic.

"Leave her alone," I told Damien.

"I'm not doing anything to her," he replied.

In fact, he did nothing but hover in her vicinity and make rather trite remarks. And always she stood up nervously and left, in a tell-tale way, going towards the nearest exit—the terrace of the casino, the french window of the salon, a garden gate. He needed no stronger hint and vacated the place. When she returned, she inexplicably looked for him; to be exact, I divined it from the way the nostrils of her perfect little nose flared and the impatience with which she pushed aside the empty chairs in her way. Watching her was what made me believe that all of us in that man's presence scented a delightful something, if I may flatter the atmosphere surrounding

[65]

him by associating it with the most aristocratic of our five senses, the olfactory.

What happened later was the usual thing: the two, of course, became lovers, and the young woman was alternately radiant and pale, unsociable and gay, visibly haggard so long as she resisted, dashingly rejuvenated when she stopped resisting. And when the hour struck that indicated, according to Damien and his particular religion, that "it was really necessary" for the affair to end, she vanished as if Damien had thrown her into a well.

No doubt in describing him I am slurring the character of this dispenser of pleasure, ill recompensed and probably quite incapable, if he had so desired, of giving any woman lasting happiness.

In his own way he also went "too far" when he accorded unlimited credit to the sensual satisfaction that he gave. Can his obsession with potency ever equal, for a lover, his obsession with impotence?

And what would he have said had he ever met the woman who, out of sheer generosity, fools the man by simulating ecstasy? But I need not worry on that score: most surely he encountered Charlotte, and perhaps more than once.

She produced for him her little broken cries, while she turned her head aside, and while her hair veiled her forehead, her cheek, her half-shut eyes, lucid and attentive to her master's pleasure ... The Charlottes of this world nearly always have long hair.

At a time when I was—or thought I was—insensible to Damien's attraction, I suggested that he and I go for a voyage together, a pair of courteously egotistic companions, accommodating, fond of long silences . . .

"I only like to travel with women," he replied.

His gentle tone was meant to soften the brutal remark. But, afraid he had offended me, he dressed it up with a remark that was even worse.

"You, a woman? Why, try as you will . . ."

# FOUR

A CHAMPION, when defeated by another champion, is none the less ready to applaud a superior speed, an innate ability to cut the air and cover distance. Damien's remark hurt me for quite a while, and since it happened to be one of the last remarks he ever made to me, I never had the opportunity to admit to him that, oddly enough, I was secretly craving just then to be completely a woman. I am not alluding to a former self, a public and legendary figure that I had ostentatiously cultivated and arranged as to costume and external details. I am alluding to a genuine mental hermaphroditism which burdens certain highly complex human beings. And if Damien's pronouncement vexed me, it was because I happened to be making a particular effort at the time to rid myself of this ambiguity, along with all its flaws and privileges, and to offer them up, still warm, at the feet of a certain man to whom I offered a healthy and quite female body and its perhaps fallacious vocation of servant. But as for the man, he was not taken in; he had detected the masculine streak in my character by some trait of mine I could not identify, and, though tempted, had fled. Later he returned, full of grudges and mistrust. And I did not as yet think to put to use the warning Damien had given me.

[68]

Of what avail is it to warn the blind? The blind trust only their own well-known infallibility and are determined to assume the full responsibility of hurting themselves. Thus I hurt myself in my own stupid and forthright way.

"There's no reason to be so upset," Marguerite Moreno said to me one day. "Why don't you just accept the fact that for certain men some women represent a risk of homosexuality?"

"You and I may comfort ourselves with that thought, Marguerite, at any rate. But if what you say is true, who will realize that we are women?"

"Other women. Women aren't offended or deluded by our masculine wit. Think it over . . ."

I interrupted her with a gesture. We had the comfortable habit of leaving a sentence hanging midway as soon as one of us had grasped the point. Marguerite Moreno thought I stopped her now out of decency, and she fell silent. No one can imagine the number of subjects, the amount of words that are left out of the conversation of two women who can talk to each other with absolute freedom. They can allow themselves the luxury of choosing what to say.

"A great many men have a feminine streak in their mental make-up," Moreno continued. "I emphasize: in their mental make-up."

"I quite understood," I said gloomily.

"Because, when it comes to morals, they are unassailable, they are quite strict, as a matter of fact!"

Amused, I nodded in agreement.

". . . And they are gallant souls, in the general acceptance of the term, the military way of using it. But oh, how they shriek if a caterpillar grazes them or if a bee flies too close; and just notice how they go pale at the very sight of a big black cockroach or the cockroach's cousin, the earwig . . ."

"Them? Are they all that numerous, Marguerite?"

She bowed her head with that grave, donnish air that people who have seen her films find so comic.

"And what about us? What about us women who constitute their homosexual risk? Are we equally numerous?"

"Far from it, I'm sorry to say. With an equal, even an equal in number, one can always get along. I've not finished. I've got only as far as the cockroach. But haven't you noticed, when *they* let themselves go in a violent scene with a woman, haven't you noticed that they never forget to keep their eyes averted from the face of the woman they're blackguarding, and focus on her hands?"

"And if they're quarrelling with a man?"

"They never make scenes with another man. They may despise and fear the other man, but rather than be obliged to exchange words with him, they prefer to have it out in a duel."

I burst out laughing—it does one good, when at a safe distance from the claws that have wounded us, to laugh at them, even when the old wounds are still raw and gaping.

"In short," the clairvoyant continued, "if they are often deluded by the expression on our face, they can more safely consult, behind us, the expression on our back . . .

[70]

Oh, how beautifully they laugh, and how easily they weep!"

She uttered a Spanish oath and made a face at some memory or other. Then she yawned and succumbed to sleep, leaning her head against the high-backed arm-chair. Her strong, sexless features softened a little as she sank into the sudden sleep of all trained workers, who know how to recoup their strength by taking a ten-minute nap in the bus or the Métro, a quarter of an hour at rehearsals as they sit on the tabouret that will serve in one scene as a Regency desk and in the next will represent a flowering hedge, or beneath the tropical lights of the cinema studios. Sitting or leaning, they sleep the sleep of the careworn, the weary, the conscientious worker. Asleep, she rather resembled Dante, or a refined hidalgo, or Leonardo da Vinci's Saint John the Baptist. Now that our woman's wealth of hair is shorn, when our breasts and hands and stomach are hidden, what remains of our feminine exteriors? Sleep brings an incalculable number of women to assume the form they would no doubt have chosen if their waking state did not keep them in ignorance of themselves. The same applies to men . . . Oh, the charm of a sleeping man, how vividly I recall it! From forehead to mouth he was, behind his closed eyelids, all smiles, with the arch nonchalance of a sultana behind a barred window. And I who would willingly have been completely woman, completely and stupidly female, with what male wistfulness did I gaze at that man who had such a delightful laugh and who could respond to a beautiful poem or landscape . . .

[71]

That man always comes into our lives more than once. His second apparition is less frightening, for we had thought him unique in the art of pleasing and destroying; by reappearing, he loses stature.

Grudgingly we confer upon him generous and noble attributes and make the inevitable gestures to which he has the right, we employ an anthropometry that renders him commonplace. Fashioned for the use and the hostility of woman, he none the less recognizes at a distance, in a man, his own species and the amiable peril his own species represents, and so he steps aside. For he knows that he is stripped of his powers the minute a woman, in talking about him, should say "they" instead of "he" . . .

"Isn't it a fact, Marguerite, that a standardized executioner . . ."

But Marguerite Moreno was sleeping, her conquistador nose turned towards adventure. Her deep sleep gave to her mouth, small and firm in her waking state, a plaintive look of submission.

Cautiously I reached for a light coverlet and laid it over Chimène and Le Cid, closely united in the sleep of a single body. Then I resumed my post at the side of a worktable, where my woman's eyes followed, on the pale blue bonded paper, the hard and stubby hand of a gardener writing.

A woman needs a fine and rare sincerity and a good amount of high-minded simplicity to determine what it is in her that tips the scale and adds some standard and approved element to her clandestine sex life. Sincerity is not a spontaneous flower, nor is modesty either.

Damien was the first to designate, in a word, my place in the scheme of things. I believe he assigned to me the place of a spectator; he felt I should have one of those choice seats that allow the spectator, when excited, to rush out on the stage and, duly staggering, join the actors and take part in what is going on.

I was not long deluded by those photographs that show me wearing a stiff mannish collar, necktie, short jacket over a straight skirt, a lighted cigarette between two fingers. Certainly I turned on them a less penetrating look than did that arrant old demon of painting, Boldini. I saw him for the first time in his studio, where the gown of a big unfinished portrait of a woman, a satin gown of blinding white—peppermint-lozenge white—caught and flashed back all the light in the room. Boldini turned his griffin face away from the portrait and gave me a deliberate stare.

"Are you the one," he said, "who puts on a dinner jacket in the evening?"

"I may have done so, for a costume party."

"You're the one who plays the mime?"

"Yes."

"And you're the one who goes on stage without tights? And who dances—*così, così*—quite naked?"

"I beg your pardon! I've never appeared naked on any stage. It may have been said, and said in print, but the truth is . . ."

He was not even listening. He laughed, shrewdly, insinuatingly, and patted my cheek.

[73]

"My, what a proper young lady we are," he murmured, "what a proper young lady we are!"

At once he forgot me and returned to his work, expending, for the benefit of the peppermint-lozenge painting, his demoniac energy in froglike leaps, gurgles, shrieks, in magical brush strokes, in Italian ballads, and in monologues.

"A grreat meestake! A grreat meestake!" he yelped suddenly.

He leaped backward, eyed the "meestake", recovered his energy and gave it, as if by surprise, a subtle lick of the brush.

". . . Meeraculously co-rect-ed!"

He paid no more attention to me. An empty gown, lacklustre, not quite white, was posing for him on an armchair. It was from that dull gown that he was creating on the canvas, stroke by stroke, the whites of cream, of snow, of glazed paper, of new metal, the white of the unfathomable, and the white of bonbons, a tour de force of whites . . . I remember that my dog Toby trembled against my legs; he already knew more than I did, certainly, about the misshapen divinity who was leaping about there in front of us . . .

The "proper young lady", offended, took dignified leave, adjusted the knot of a mannish necktie that had been imported from London, and went away, looking as much as possible like a bad boy, to rejoin a strange company of women who led a marginal and timorous life, sustained by an out-of-date form of snobbishness.

How timid I was, at that period when I was trying to

[74]

look like a boy, and how feminine I was beneath my disguise of cropped hair. "Who would take us to be women? Why, women." They alone were not fooled. With such distinguishing marks as pleated shirt front, hard collar, sometimes a waistcoat, and always a silk pocket handkerchief, I frequented a society perishing on the margin of all societies. Although morals, good and bad, have not changed during the past twenty-five or thirty years, class consciousness, in destroying itself, has gradually undermined and debilitated the clique I am referring to, which tried, trembling with fear, to live without hypocrisy, the breathable air of society. This clique, or sect, claimed the right of "personal freedom" and equality with homosexuality, that imperturbable establishment. And they scoffed, if in whispers, at "Papa" Lépine, the Prefect of Police, who never could take lightly the question of women in men's clothes. The adherents of this clique of women exacted secrecy for their parties, where they appeared dressed in long trousers and dinner jackets and behaved with unsurpassed propriety. They tried to reserve for themselves certain bars and restaurants and to enjoy there the guilty pleasures of backgammon and bezique. Then they gave up the struggle, and the sect's most stubborn proselytes never crossed the street or left their carriage without putting on, heart pounding, a long, plain cloak which gave them an excessively respectable look and effectively concealed their masculine attire.

At the home of the best-known woman among them— the best known and the most misunderstood—fine wines, long cigars, photographs of a smartly-turned-out horseman, one or two languorous portraits of very pretty women, bespoke the sensual and rakish life of a bachelor. But the lady of the house, in dark masculine attire, belied any idea of gaiety or bravado. Pale, without blemish or blush, pale like certain antique Roman marbles that seem steeped in light, the sound of her voice muffled and sweet, she had all the ease and good manners of a man, the restrained gestures, the virile poise of a man. Her married name, when I knew her, was still disturbing. Her friends, as well as her enemies, never referred to her except by her title and a charming Christian name, title and name alike clashing with her stocky masculine physique and reserved, almost shy manner. From the highest strata of society, La Chevalière, as we shall call her, was having her fling, sowing her wild oats like a prince. And like a prince, she had her counterparts. Napoleon III gave us Georges Ville, who survived him for a long time. La Chevalière could not prevent this man-woman, deathly pale, powdered, self-assertive, from exhibiting herself and signing the same initials as her model.

Where could I find, nowadays, messmates like those who, gathered around La Chevalière, emptied her wine cellar and her purse? Baronesses of the Empire, canonesses, lady cousins of Czars, illegitimate daughters of grand-dukes, exquisites of the Parisian bourgeoisie, and also some aged horsewomen of the Austrian aristocracy, hand and eye of steel ... Some of these ladies fondly kept in their protective and jealous shadow women younger than they, clever young actresses, the next to the last authentic demi-mondaine of the epoch, a music-hall star

[76]

... You heard them in whispered conversation, but to the great disappointment of the curious ear, the dialogue was banal. "How did your lesson go? Do you have it now, your Chopin waltz?" "Take your furs off here, you will get hot and won't be in voice this evening. Yes, you know better than I do, of course. But I studied with Nilsson, please remember that, my dear ..." "Tut, tut, my sweet, one doesn't cut a baba with a knife ... Take a small fork ..." "You have no idea of time, and if I didn't think for you, my pet ... What do you mean by putting your husband into a bad humour by going home late every time?"

Among these women, free yet timorous, addicted to late hours, darkened rooms, gambling, and indolence, I almost never detected a trace of cynicism. Sparing of words, all they needed was an allusion. I heard one of them, one only —a German princess with the fresh chubby face of a butcher boy—introduce her *petite amie* one day as "my spouse", whereupon my blunt gentlemen in skirts wrinkled their noses in distaste and pretended not to hear. "It's not that I conceal anything," briefly commented the Vicomtesse de X. "It's simply that I don't like showing off."

It was otherwise with their protégées, who were, more often than not, rather rude young creatures, insinuating and grasping. Not surprising, this, for these ladies in male attire had, by birth and from infancy, a taste for below-stairs accomplices and comrades-in-livery—and, as a consequence, an incurable timidity, which they dissimulated as best they could. Pride in giving pleasure relieved them of the need for any other dignity; they tolerated being

[77]

addressed familiarly by these young creatures and found again, beneath the insult, the tremulous and secret pleasure of their childhood when dining at the servants' table.

In the servants' quarters, from their first toddling steps, they had found their allies and their tormentors, whom they and their brothers equally feared and loved. It is quite necessary for a child to love. The women of whom I am speaking were considerably older than I, they had grown up in an epoch when the aristocracy, even more than the rich bourgeoisie, handed over their progeny to the domestic staff. It is a question who was worth more to the children, the paid tormentor or the depraved ally. My narrators did not judge them. They did not bother to embroider their tales but calmly described the orgies in the pantry, when strong liquor was poured out for the dazed children, or told how those underlings would one day stuff the babies with food and next day forget to feed them at all ... They did not speak in the maudlin tone of cheap journalism; none of these women claimed the grade of infant martyr, not even the daughter of the Duke de X, who said that from six to fifteen she had never worn a pair of new shoes, that her shoes had all been hand-me-downs from her elder brother or sister, and with holes in the soles. Blandly, and at times rather mockingly, she described incidents of her childhood.

"In the corridor outside our nursery," she related, "was a small antique lady's desk in rosewood, incrusted with a large medallion in Sèvres porcelain, with the monogram of a queen and her crown glittering in diamonds. My mother did not like that small piece of furniture and had sentenced it to exile in the corridor, where it stood between two doors. Well, to please my mother, when we dressed for dinner we always set our muddy shoes on the top of that *bonheur-du-jour*, right on the Sèvres medallion and its diamonds . . ."

Married to a man she hated, my narrator had not dared to confess her despair when she fancied she was pregnant, except to an old footman, an ancient corrupter of princelings, a valet she feared.

"He brought me a concoction to drink," she said, touched at the recollection. "He, and he alone in the world, pitied me . . . What he gave me to drink was pretty horrible . . . I remember that I wept . . ."

"With grief?"

"No. I cried because, while I swallowed that horror, the old fellow tried to hearten me by calling me *niña* and *pobrecita*, just as he had when I was a child."

These women who had been dispossessed of their rightful childhoods and who, as girls, had been more than orphans, were now in their maturity the fond instructors of a younger generation. They never seemed ridiculous to me. Yet some of them wore a monocle, a white carnation in the buttonhole, took the name of God in vain, and discussed horses competently. These mannish women I am calling to mind were, indeed, almost as fond of the horse, that warm, enigmatic, stubborn, and sensitive creature, as they were of their young protégées. With their strong slender hands they were able to break in and subjugate a horse, and when age and hard times deprived them of the whip and the hunting crop, they lost their final sceptre.

[79]

A garage, no matter how elegant, can never equal the smartness of a stable. The motor car cannot be mounted; a mechanical carriage bestows no psychological glamour on its driver. But the dust of the bridle paths in the Bois still haloes, in countless memories, those equestriennes who did not need to ride astride to assert their ambiguity.

Seated on the handsome back of a lean thoroughbred, mounted on the twin pedestal of a chestnut crupper, where shimmered two ellipses of unctuous light, they were freed of the awkward, toed-out stance of the ballet dancer that marred their walk. The thing women in men's clothes imitate worst is a man's stride. "They raise their knees too high, they don't tuck in their bottoms as they should," was the severe pronouncement of La Chevalière. The exciting scent of horses, that so masculine odour, never quite left these women, but lingered on after the ride. I saw and hailed the decline of these women. They tried to describe and explain their vanished charm. They tried to render intelligible for us their success with women and their defiant taste for women. The astonishing thing is that they managed to do so. I am not referring here to La Chevalière, who by character as well as physique was above them. Restless and uncertain in her pursuit of love, she searched with her anxious eyes, so dark they were almost black beneath a low, white forehead, for what she never found: a settled and sentimental attachment. For more than forty years, this woman with the bearing of a handsome boy endured the pride and punishment of never being able to establish a real and lasting affair with a woman. It was not for lack of trying, because she asked nothing better or worse. But the salacious expectations of women shocked her very natural platonic tendencies, which resembled more the suppressed excitement, the diffuse emotion of an adolescent, than a woman's explicit need. Twenty years ago she tried, with bitterness, to explain herself to me. "I do not know anything about completeness in love," she said, "except the *idea* I have of it. But they, the women, have never allowed me to stop at that point . . ."

"Without exception?"

"Without exception."

"Why?"

"I'm sure I don't know."

La Chevalière shrugged. The expression that appeared on her face recalled for a minute Damien's expression when he had assured me that "women go too far . . ." Like Damien, she seemed to be recalling something rather sad, rather repellent, and she was about to say more, but like him she contained herself.

"I'm sure I don't know," she repeated.

"But what in heaven's name do they hope for, by going further? Do they give so much credit to the physical act, the idea of the paroxysm of pleasure?"

"No doubt," she said, uncertainly.

"They must at least have an opinion on that special pleasure? Do they fling themselves upon it as upon a panacea, do they see in it a kind of consecration? Do they demand it, or accept it, more simply, as a proof of mutual trust?"

La Chevalière averted her eyes, flicked off the long ash

[81]

on her cigar, waved her hand as a discreet man might do.

"This is beyond me," she said. "It does not even concern me."

"And yet . . ."

She repeated her gesture and smiled to dissuade me from persisting.

"I'm of the opinion," she said, "that in the ancient Nativities the portrait of the 'donor' occupies far too much space in the picture . . ."

La Chevalière always had, still has wit, a quick sense of repartee. The years have made little change in her and have let her keep her smile, which is so difficult to depict, so difficult to forget. That smile of the "donor" who despises his gifts did not, however, discourage me from questioning her. But she was shy and rejected this subject of conversation, to which, however, I will add a remark she let fall one day when an ugly young woman was being described in detail in her hearing.

"That girl, if she didn't have her two eyes . . ."

"What more does a woman need besides her two eyes?" asked La Chevalière.

In effect, I knew she was mad about blue-green eyes, and when I told her she shared with Jean Lorrain the obsession of "green" eyes, she was annoyed.

"Oh," she said, "but it's not the same thing at all! Jean Lorrain takes off from green eyes to go . . . you know where. He's a man for whom 'the deep calleth to deep'. . ."

The remark is worth more than her epoch and the literature of the turn of the century, swollen with masks

[82]

and voodoo, black masses, blissful decapitated women whose heads float among narcissi and blue toads. For a timid soul, exalted in silence and perpetually adolescent, what more seductive depths could one plunge into than the eyes of the loved one, and descend in thought and blissfully lose one's life between the seaweed and the star?

The seduction emanating from a person of uncertain or dissimulated sex is powerful. Those who have never experienced it liken it to the banal attraction of the love that evicts the male element. This is a gross misconception. Anxious and veiled, never exposed to the light of day, the androgynous creature wanders, wonders, and implores in a whisper . . . Its half equal, man, is soon scared and flees. There remains its half equal, a woman. There especially remains for the androgynous creature the right, even the obligation, never to be happy. If jovial, the androgynous creature is a monster. But it trails irrevocably among us its seraphic suffering, its glimmering tears. It goes from a tender inclination to maternal adoption . . . As I write this, I am thinking of La Chevalière. It was she who most often bruised herself in a collision with a woman—a woman, that whispering guide, presumptuous, strangely explicit, who took her by the hand and said, "Come, I will help you find yourself . . ."

"I am neither that nor anything else, alas," said La Chevalière, dropping the vicious little hand. "What I lack cannot be found by searching for it."

She is the person who has no counterpart anywhere. At one time she believed that she had her counterpart in the features of a young woman, and again in the features of a

handsome young man—yes, of a young man, why not?—
so handsome that love seemed to despair of him, and who,
moreover, clung to no one. He gave to La Chevalière a
name that made her blush with joy and gratitude: he
called her "my father". But she soon saw that again she
had been mistaken, that one can adopt only the child one
has begotten . . .

"All the same," the solitary woman sighs at times, "I
must not complain, I shall have been a mirage . . ."

Around her, beneath her, a quarrelsome and timid life
gravitated. She served as the ideal, as the target, and
ignored the fact. She was praised, she was slandered, her
name was repeated in the midst of a subdued and almost
subterranean tumult, was heard especially in the friendly
little dives, the tiny, neighbourhood cinemas frequented
by groups of her women friends—basement rooms arranged as restaurants, dim, and blue with tobacco smoke.
There was also a cellar in Montmartre that welcomed
these uneasy women, haunted by their own solitude, who
felt safe within the low-ceilinged room beneath the eye of
a frank proprietress who shared their predilections, while
an unctuous and authentic cheese fondue sputtered and
the loud contralto of an artiste, one of their familiars, sang
to them the romantic ballads of Augusta Holmès . . . The
same need for a refuge, warmth, and darkness, the same
fear of intruders and sightseers assembled here these
women whose faces, if not their names, soon became
familiar to me. Literature and the makers of literature
were absent from these gatherings and I delighted in that
absence, along with the empty gaiety of the chatter and

[84]

the diverting and challenging exchange of glances, the cryptic reference to certain treasons, comprehended at once, and the sudden outbursts of ferocity. I revelled in the admirable quickness of their half-spoken language, the exchange of threats, of promises, as if, once the slow-thinking male had been banished, every message from woman to woman became clear and overwhelming, restricted to a small but infallible number of signs ...

All amours tend to create a dead-end atmosphere. "There! It's finished, we've arrived, and beyond us two there is nothing now, not even an opening for escape," murmurs one woman to her protégée, using the language of a lover. And as a proof, she indicates the low ceiling, the dim light, the women who are their counterparts, making her listen to the masculine rumble of the outside world and hear how it is reduced to the booming of a distant danger.

# FIVE

I STILL HAVE IN MY POSSESSION some thirty letters Pauline Tarn wrote to me. I had a great many more, but some of them were filched from me, and the shortest, the least attractive, I gave away to "fans" of Renée Vivien. A few of them, too, have been mislaid.

If I were to publish the correspondence of this poet who never ceased claiming kinship with Lesbos, it would astound only because of its childishness. I stress this very particular childish quality, which strikes a false note— dare I say a note of obvious insincerity? The charming face of Renée Vivien reflected only a part of that childlike quality, in the rounded cheek, soft and downy, in the innocent short upper lip, so typically English, curled up and revealing four little front teeth. A bright smile constantly lit up her eyes, a chestnut-brown which became greenish in sunlight. She wore her long, beautiful ash-blond hair, which was fine and straight, massed at the top of her head, from which stray locks came down now and then like wisps of fine straw.

There is not a single feature of her youthful face that I do not vividly recall. Everything in it bespoke childishness, roguishness, and the propensity to laughter. Impossible to find anywhere in that face, from the fair hair to the sweet dimple of the weak little chin, any line that was not a line of laughter, any sign of the hidden tragic melancholy that throbs in the poetry of Renée Vivien. I never saw Renée sad. She would exclaim, in her lisping English accent, "Oh, my dear little Colette, how disgusting this life is!" Then she would burst into laughter. In all too many of her notes, I find that same exclamation repeated, often spelled out frankly in the coarsest words: "Isn't this life sheer muck? Well, I hope it will soon be over!" This impatience of hers amused her friends, but her hope was not dashed, for she died in her thirtieth year.

Our friendship was in no way literary, it goes without saying—or rather, I should say, thanks to my respect for literature. I am sparing of words on that subject, except for occasional exclamations of admiration, and in Renée Vivien I found the same diffidence and well-bred restraint. She, too, refused to "talk shop". Whenever she gave me any of her books, she always hid them under a bouquet of violets or a basket of fruit or a length of Oriental silk. She was secretive with me on the two literary aspects of her brief existence: the cause of her sadness, and her method of work. Where did she work? And at what hours? The vast, dark, sumptuous, and ever changing flat in the avenue du Bois gave no hint of work. That ground-floor flat in the avenue du Bois has never been well described, by the way. Except for some gigantic Buddhas, all the furnishings moved mysteriously: after provoking surprise and admiration for a time, they had a way of disappearing . . .

[87]

Among the unstable marvels, Renée wandered, not so much clad as veiled in black or purple, almost invisible in the scented darkness of the immense rooms barricaded with leaded windows, the air heavy with curtains and incense. Three or four times I caught her curled up in a corner of a divan, scribbling with a pencil on a writing-pad propped on her knees. On these occasions she always sprang up guiltily, excusing herself, murmuring, "It's nothing, I've finished now . . ." Her lithe body devoid of density languidly drooped, as if beneath the weight of her poppy-flower head with its pale golden hair, surmounted by immense and unsteady hats. She held her long and slender hands in front of her, gropingly. The dresses she wore were always long, covering her feet, and she was afflicted with an angelic clumsiness, was always losing as she went her gloves, handkerchief, sunshade, scarf . . .

She was constantly giving things away: the bracelets on her arms opened up, the necklace slipped from her martyr's throat. She was as if deciduous. It was as if her languorous body rejected anything that would give it a third dimension.

The first time I dined at her place, three brown tapers dripped waxen tears in tall candlesticks and did not dispel the gloom. A low table, from the Orient, offered a pell-mell assortment of *les hors d'œuvre*—strips of raw fish rolled upon glass wands, *foie gras*, shrimps, salad seasoned with sugar and pepper—and there was a well-chosen Piper-Heidsieck champagne *brut*, and very strong cock-tails—Renée Vivien was ahead of her time. Suffocated with the obscurity, mistrustful of the unfamiliar fire of

[88]

Russian, Greek, and Chinese alcohols, I scarcely touched the food. I remember that Renée's gay laughter, her liveliness, the faint halo of light trembling in her golden hair all combined to sadden me, as does the happiness of blind children who laugh and play without the help of light. I did not believe that this meeting in this luxurious flat submerged in darkness could result in any real friendship with this tall young woman who tossed off her drink with the obliviousness one sees in bridesmaids at a country wedding.

Among the beverages that she raised to her lips was a cloudy elixir in which floated a cherry harpooned on a toothpick. I laid a hand on her arm and cautioned her.

"Don't drink it."

She opened her eyes so wide that the lashes of her upper eyelids touched her eyebrows.

"Why not?"

"I've tasted it," I said, embarrassed. "It's . . . it's deadly. Be careful, it tastes like some kind of vitriol."

I dared not tell her that I suspected a practical joke. She laughed, flashing her white teeth.

"But these are my own cocktails, *ma pethith Coletthe.* They are excellent."

She emptied the glass at one gulp, neither gasping nor blinking, and her rounded cheek kept its floral pallor.

I did not notice that evening her almost total abstention from food, but later on I discovered that she subsisted mainly on a few spoonfuls of rice, some fruit or other, and alcohol—especially alcohol. During this first evening,

[89]

nothing could dispel the uneasiness engendered by the strangeness of the place, bound to astonish a guest, the semi-darkness, the exotic foods on plates of jade, vermeil, or Chinese porcelain, foods that had come from countries too far away.

However, I was to see Renée Vivien many times afterwards.

We discovered that her house and mine communicated, thanks to the two garden courts separated only by a grille, and that the concierge who had the keys was not incorruptible; I could therefore go from the rue de Villejust to the avenue du Bois to visit her without setting foot in the street. Occasionally I used this facility. On my way, I would rap on the windows of the garden flat where Robert d'Humières lived, and he would open his window and hold out an immaculate treasure, an armful of snow, that is to say, his blue-eyed white cat, Lanka, saying, "To you I entrust my most precious possession."

Twenty metres farther on, and I would confront, at Renée's, the air which, like stagnant water, slowed down my steps, the odour of incense, of flowers, of overripe apples. It is an understatement to say that I was stifled in that gloom. I became almost wickedly intolerant there, yet never wore out the patience of the gossamer angel who dedicated offerings of lady apples to the Buddhas. One day, when the spring wind was stripping the leaves from the Judas trees in the avenue, I was nauseated by the funereal perfumes and tried to open the window: it was nailed shut. What a contribution such a detail is, what a flourish it adds to a theme already rich! What a quantity of lurid gleams and glints of gold in the semi-darkness, of whispering voices behind the doors, of Chinese masks, of ancient instruments hanging on the walls, mute, only vaguely whimpering, at the banging of a door beneath my heavy hand. At Renée Vivien's I could have wished to be younger, so I could be a little fearful. But impatience got the better of me and one evening I brought an offending, an inadmissible big oil lamp, and plumped it down, lit, in front of my plate. Renée wept big tears over this, like a child—it is only right to add that she consoled herself in like manner.

Try as she would to please me by inviting along with me two or three of my best friends, to make me happy, our intimacy did not seem to make any real progress. At the table in the darkness, or lounging comfortably and provided with exotic food and drink, Turkish cigarettes or Chinese blond tobacco in miniature silver pipes, we remained a bit stiff and uneasy, as if our young hostess and we ourselves apprehended the unexpected return of an absent and unknown "master".

This "master" was never referred to by the name of woman. We seemed to be waiting for some catastrophe to project her into our midst, but she merely kept sending invisible messengers laden with jades, enamels, lacquers, fabrics . . . A collection of ancient Persian gold coins came, glittered, disappeared, leaving in its place glass cabinets of exotic butterflies and other insects, which in their turn gave way to a colossal Buddha, a miniature garden of bushes having leaves of crystal and fruit of precious stones. From one marvel to another Renée moved, uncertainly,

[91]

already detached, and showing the indifferent self-efface-ment of a guard in a museum.

When I recall the changes which gradually rendered Renée more understandable, I believe I can link these with certain gestures at first, then with some words that threw a different light on her. Some people become transformed by riches, others acquire a real life only by impoverish-ment, their very destitution giving them life. When was I able to forget that Renée Vivien was a poet, I mean, when did I begin to feel a real interest in her? No doubt it was one evening when dining at her place, an evening of spicy foods and of disquieting drinks—I risked drinking only two glasses of a perfect and very dry champagne—a gay evening and yet inexplicably strained, when Renée's gaiety expressed itself in laughter, in an eagerness to applaud exaggeratedly any least droll word.

Exceptionally that evening she wore a white dress that bared her delicate and youthful throat and the nape of her neck, where wisps of her soft straight hair were always coming undone. Between two remarks and without warn-ing, she suddenly leaned against the back of her chair, her head bowed, her chin on her thin chest, her eyes closed . . . I can still see her two slender hands resting open and lifeless on the tablecloth.

This fainting spell, or whatever it was, lasted less than ten seconds, and Renée came to without embarrassment.

"Forgive me, my dears, I must have gone to sleep," she murmured, and resumed the argument she had left for the fleeting death from which she had returned fired with a strange frenzy.

[92]

"Oh, that B.!" she exclaimed, "I don't want to hear any more about him or his verses tonight. He has *no* talent. He is—wait, I know what he is, he's a cunt, a cunt with a pen. Yes, a cunt with a pen!"

The word fell into our silence, coarse, blunt. Anyone of us would have been capable of pronouncing that word in an undertone and among ourselves, but as Renée repeated the indecent remark, there reigned on her childlike features a blank expression that set the words outside time, deprived of any significance, and revealed in the speaker a profound disorder.

The wily lunatic is lost if through the narrowest crack he allows a sane eye to peer into his locked universe and thus profane it. Afterwards, it is the sane eye that changes, is affected, becomes fascinated with the mystery it has seen and can never cease to question. The more sensitive the lunatic, the less able is he to resist this prying interest of the normal human being. I felt that Renée's change of key —to myself, I compared Renée to a sweet melody, a little flat despite its laborious harmonies—was approaching.

At Pascaud's, where we had gone to hire costumes for the fancy-dress ball Robert d'Humières was giving at the Théâtre des Arts, which he directed, Renée Vivien, as she dressed again after the fitting of her costume—she intended to go as Jane Grey on the executioner's block, exactly, alas, as Paul Delaroche painted her—put on by mistake my black coat instead of her own.

"It almost fits you," I said, laughing. "But for you to look your best in it, something is needed here, and here ... Otherwise . . ."

"It almost fits me?" Renée repeated.

I can still see how her face clouded, how her mouth fell open in stunned surprise.

"It's a great misfortune," she stammered, "a great misfortune that you've just announced to me . . ."

She turned a gloomy and calculating look upon me—at that period I was a pleasant little cob pony of a person—then rapidly collected herself and we separated. That evening I was handed a letter she had addressed to me and my friends who were to figure in the *tableau vivant* of Jane Grey. It read:

> *My dears, the worst possible thing has happened to me: I've carelessly put on weight—ten pounds. But there are still ten days before our ball, in which I can lose them—that's enough, it's got to be enough, for I must not, at any price, weigh more than fifty-two kilos. Don't try to find me, I'm going to a place none of you knows. Count on me, I'll be back in ten days, and all ready for the ball. Yours, Renée.*

She kept her word. We heard later on that she had spent the ten days at the Pavillon Henri IV in Saint-Germain. In the mornings she drank a glass of tea, then walked in the forest until her strength gave out. Then she drank more tea, this time with alcohol added, and went to bed in an almost fainting condition. Next day it began all over again. She had the inexhaustible strength of unbalanced people. "We walked perhaps twenty kilometres every day," her companion confessed to us later on. "I don't know how mademoiselle kept going. As for myself, I ate normally, yet was exhausted."

The ten days over with, Renée met us at eleven o'clock in the evening at the Théâtre des Arts. She looked very pretty in her costume, powdered and rouged, hollow-eyed, her hair loose on one shoulder, and she was gay in a distracted kind of way. She still had the strength to play the part of Jane Grey, her hands tied, her bowed head revealing a white nape, her fair hair flooding out on the block. But afterwards she fainted backstage, the victim of the saddest and most violent case of alcohol poisoning, aggravated by starvation and some drug or other.

This was her very pathetic secret, the confession of a quite ordinary neurosis. Or was it? Yes, if one can be satisfied with a single fact, as I was for a time—a rather short time. Renée was dying when I was told how she had managed in a weirdly simple way to drink to excess without out anyone in Paris or anyone in Nice in the little house in the Parc Cessole ever being able to catch her at it . . .

Adjoining the bathroom, in a small room that substi-tuted as a linen closet, her docile chambermaid sat sewing. Quick, maladroit, stumbling against the furniture, Renée was constantly calling out for help to . . . let us call her Justine, for that was absolutely not her name.

"Justine, my dear, will you sew on this hook that's come off?" "Justine, dear, have you ironed my embroi-dered frock?" "Quick, my slipper ribbon is undone . . ." "Oh! These new gloves still have a price tag on, do take it off, Justine, will you?" "Please, Justine, tell the cook that tonight . . ."

Behind the sewing-room door, which remained open, you heard only a murmured reply: "Yes, mademoiselle. Very well, mademoiselle . . ." And the maid did not leave the chair where she sat at work. Every time Renée appeared, Justine had only to lean over to reach, under her chair, one of the filled wineglasses that her skirt concealed. She held it out in silence to Renée, who emptied it at a gulp and went from the linen closet to the bathroom, where she found waiting her, punctually renewed, a glass of milky-looking water clouded with perfumes. She would gargle this and hurriedly spit it out. People who had seen and smelled that glass of perfumed liquid believed and have affirmed that Renée Vivien drank toilet water. What she so foolishly imbibed was no better.

I sometimes met Renée in the mornings, when I led my memorable cat Prrou out on a leash for a walk along the grassy paths in the avenue du Bois, and I recall one such encounter. As usual when she ventured out into the streets, Renée was a bit overdressed. In getting into the carriage that morning, she stepped on the hem of her long skirt and caught the strap of her bag on the handle of the door.

"Where are you going this early in the day?" I asked.

"To buy my Buddha. I've decided to buy one every day. Don't you think that's a good idea?"

"Excellent. Enjoy yourself!"

She turned to wave good-bye and knocked her hat askew. To hold it on, she raised the hand she had passed through the strap of the bag and it, ill shut, fell open, scattering a quantity of crumpled banknotes. "Oh, *mon*

[96]

*Dieu*," she exclaimed, laughing softly. At last the fiacre, the big hat, the dress with the ripped hem went off in the distance, while, close to my cat hygienically scratching the grass, I stood reflecting: "The alcohol . . . the thinness . . . the poetry, the daily Buddha . . . And that's not all. What is the dark origin of all this nonsense?"

May I be excused for having included as an element of "all this nonsense" the word "poetry". Renée Vivien has left a great many poems of unequal strength, force, merit, unequal as the human breath, as the pulsations of human suffering. The cult of which they sing arouses curiosity and then infatuation; today they have disarmed the indignation of even the lowest kind of moralists—and this is a fate I would not have dared to promise them if they had lauded only the love of Chloë for Daphnis, since the lowest kind of moralist follows the fashions and makes a display of broadmindedness. In addition, Renée's work inhabits a region of elevated melancholy, in which the *amies*, the female couple, daydream and weep as often as they embrace. Admirably acquainted with our language, broken to the strict rules of French metre, Renée Vivien betrays her foreignness—that is to say, her assimilation of French masterworks relatively late in life—by excluding her Baudelairism in the years 1900–1909, which was rather late for us.

When I found out she was so fallible, so faddy, so enslaved to a ruinous habit that she hoped to keep secret, my instinctive attraction to Renée changed into friendship. Friendship is not always circumspect, and one day I went so far as to put a strange question.

"Tell me, Renée. Are you happy?"

Renée blushed, smiled, then abruptly stiffened.

"Why, of course, my dear Colette. Why would you want me to be unhappy?"

"I didn't say I wanted it," I retorted.

And I went off, dissatisfied with us both. But next day her embarrassed laugh was apologetic and she thrashed the air around me with her long arms, maladroit and affectionate, as if she were looking for a way into my confidence. I noticed her listlessness, the dark rings under her eyes, and I asked her if she was ill.

"Why, not at all," she protested emphatically.

She then yawned behind her hand and explained the reasons for her lassitude in terms so clear that I could not believe my ears. And she did not stop there . . . What new warmth had melted her reserve and encouraged such expansiveness? Unhindered by any ambiguity, she spoke openly, and what she spoke of was not love but sexual satisfaction, and this, of course, referred to the only sexual satisfaction she knew, the pleasure she took with a woman. Then it was a question of the satisfactions of another epoch, another woman, and regrets and comparisons. Her way of talking about physical love was rather like that of little girls brought up for a life of debauchery: both innocent and crude. The most curious thing about her calm and far-fetched confessions, during the recital of which Renée never left off the tone of tranquil gossip, strangely in accord with the least ambiguous terms, was that they revealed an immodest consideration for "the senses" and the techniques of obtaining physical satisfaction ... And when, beyond the poet who praised the pallor of her Lesbian loves, their sobbing in the desolate dawns, I caught a glimpse of "Madame How-many-times" counting on her fingers, mentioning by name things and gestures, I put an end to the indiscretion of those young half-conscious lips, and not very tactfully. I believe I told Renée that certain frank remarks she had made were as suitable to her as a silk hat to a monkey ... As a sequel to this incident, I still have the brief note she sent me, very imposing in its form:

*You gravely offended me last night, Colette, and I am not one who forgives. Adieu. Renée.*

However, the other Renée, the good and charming Renée, saw to it that I had a second note two hours after the first one. It read:

*Forgive me, dear little Colette, God only knows what I wrote to you. Eat these lovely peaches as a toast to my health and come to see me. Come dine with me as soon as you can, and bring along our friends.*

I did not fail to do so, although I took exception to the odd, clandestine character of those feasts laid out among three candles, to which sometimes Renée invited a harpist, at other times a soloist. But on the threshold of her apartment, which I always said smelled like "a rich man's funeral," we met Renée in a black evening dress, ready to go out.

[99]

"No, my dears," she murmured agitatedly, "you've not made a mistake, I was expecting you tonight. Sit down at the table, I'll be back very soon, I swear it by Aphrodite! There are shrimps, *foie gras*, some Chios wine, and fruit from the Balearic Isles . . ."

In her haste, she stumbled on the steps. She turned her golden head towards me, the luminous heart of a great beehive of dark velvet, then came back to whisper in my ears: "Hush, I'm requisitioned. *She* is terrible at present."

Constrained, mystified, we remained and we waited . . . And Renée did not return.

Another time she was gaily having dinner, I mean to say, she was watching us dine, and at the dessert she stood up, gathered together with a shaky hand her long gloves, a fan, a little silk purse, then excused herself.

"My dears, I have to go . . . *Voilà* . . ."

She did not finish what she had to say but burst into tears and fled. A carriage waiting for her outside bore her away.

In spite of my old friend Hamel (called Hamond, in the *Vagabonde*), who had a paternal affection for Renée and who now interceded for her, I went home with dignity, swearing never to return. But I did return, because the friendship one has given to a human being who is already going to pieces, is already headed towards her downfall, does not obey the dictates of pride. When I went back, urged by Renée in a laconic note, I found her sitting on the rim of the tub in the cold, ugly, and rudimentary bathroom. Seeing her pallor, the trembling of her long hands, her absurd thinness encased in a black dress, I tried to cheer her by addressing her as the Muse of Lévy-Dhurmer. She paid no attention.

"I'm going away," she said.

"Yes? Where are you going?"

"I don't know. But I'm in danger. *She* will kill me. Or else *she* will take me to the other side of the world, to countries where I shall be at her mercy . . . She will kill me."

"Poison? Revolver?"

"No."

In four words she explained how she might perish. Four words of a frankness to make you blink. This would not be worth the telling, except for what Renée said then.

"With her I dare not pretend or lie, because at that moment she lays her ear over my heart."

I prefer to believe that this detail and the "danger", which both, alike, seem to have been borrowed from P. J. Toulet's *Monsieur du Paur*, were conceived under the influence of alcohol. Perhaps, even, the exhausting lesbian lover never existed. Perhaps, invisible, she owed her strength, her quasi-tangibility to the last effort, the last miracle of an imagination which, getting out of hand, brought forth ghouls instead of nymphs.

While I was on tour—the Baret Music Hall Tour—I was unaware that Renée was very close to death. She kept losing weight, always refusing to eat. In her spells of giddiness, in the aurora borealis of starvation, she thought she saw the flames of the Catholic hell. Someone close to her perhaps fanned the flames, or described them to her? Mystery. Enfeebled, she became humble and was converted. Her paganism was so little rooted in her. Fever and coughing shook her hollow chest. I was by chance spared the sight of Renée dying, then dead. She carried off with her more than one secret, and beneath her purple veil, Renée Vivien, the poet, led away—her throat encircled with moonstones, beryls, aquamarines, and other anaemic gems—the immodest child, the excited little girl who taught me, with unembarrassed competence: "There are fewer ways of making love than they say, and more than one believes . . ."

Blond, her cheek dimpled, with a tender, laughing mouth and great, soft eyes, she was, even so, drawn down beneath the earth, towards everything that is of no concern to the living. Like all those who never use their strength to the limit, I am hostile to those who let life burn them out. Voluntary consumption is, I always feel, a kind of alibi. I fear there is not much difference between the habit of obtaining sexual satisfaction and, for instance, the cigarette habit. Smokers, male and female, inject and excuse idleness in their lives every time they light a cigarette.

The habit of obtaining sexual satisfaction is less tyrannical than the tobacco habit, but it gains on one. O voluptuous pleasure, O lascivious ram, cracking your skull against all obstacles, time and again! Perhaps the only misplaced curiosity is that which persists in trying to find out here, on this side of death, what lies beyond the grave . . . Voluptuaries, consumed by their senses, always begin by flinging themselves with a great display of frenzy into an abyss. But they survive, they come to the surface again.

And they develop a routine of the abyss: "It's four o'clock ... At five I have my abyss ..." It is possible that this young woman poet, who rejected the laws of ordinary love, led a sensible enough life until her personal abyss of half-past eight in the evening. An abyss she imagined? Ghouls are rare.

## SIX

"Ghoul", "vampire"—by these names they called a
woman now dead who experienced the worst of her ill-
fame thirty-five or forty years ago. She was described to
me by an actress acquaintance, Amalia X, a former companion of mine on theatrical tours. "Ugly, but chic," was
the way Amalia X described her, adding, "She looked
very smart in a tail coat."

"Which only makes one more ill-cut masculine suit,"
I said.

Her portraits show that she was dark-complexioned,
angular, thin-lipped, displaying the insolence of a twenty-
five-year-old midinette dressed up in men's clothes on St
Catherine's Day. She was credited with having made a
number of young women wretched, of having driven one
of them to commit suicide beneath her window, of having
broken up several marriages, of having incurred rivalries
that at times ended in bloodshed. Her doorstep was heaped
with floral offerings, and she had a reputation for behaving with incomparable disdain. Well, now! So many
postulants and so few chosen? Surely that is not the bal-
ance sheet of an ogress. It looks more like the trifling
of someone who enjoyed inflicting mental cruelties. To

wreak havoc by practically abstaining from sin is not the behaviour of a vulgar woman . . .

A photograph signed with her assumed name, Lucienne de ——, shows her in correct men's evening dress, correct but with traces of bad taste, I mean to say, feminine taste. The pocket handkerchief points two inches too high; the lapels of the coat are too wide, and the style of the shoes is dubious. One feels that a feminine imagination, imprisoned beneath the bared forehead of the spurious man, regrets having been unable to let itself go in jabots, ribbons, silky fabrics. Strange, that a woman like this who rivalled and defrauded men should have as her single ambition to look and act the part of a dashing young man about town. It was hard for her to leave off her look of bravado. She dated, as did her aggressive handwriting, from the epoch of impudent cocottes. Amalia X, that good comic actress of road companies who died at the beginning of the war, had been a rival of La Lucienne in many a conquest and many a risky adventure. Amalia, if one were to believe her, had not hesitated to leave a sleeping and satiated sultan and go on foot, veiled, through the night streets of Constantinople to a hotel room where a sweet, blond, and very young woman was waiting up for her . . .

"And you must realize," the worthy Amalia confided, shuffling the pack of tarot cards on a small galvanized table in a dingy café at Tarbes or Valenciennes—I forget which—"you must realize that Constantinople then, at night, was less safe even than the boulevard de la Chapelle."

Slightly moustached, rheumatic, at the end of her strength, Amalia X still enjoyed life, was still "touring" at over sixty years of age, and recalled her past with satisfaction. "I had everything," she asserted, "beauty, happiness, misery, men, and women ... You can call it a life!" Her big handsome Israelite's eyes rolled up at the mere thought.

"But," I said, "if between your little *amie* and you there had not been the dark streets, the risks, and the old man you had just abandoned, in short, had there been no danger, would you have hurried so eagerly?"

The old comedienne looked away for a moment from the Hanged Man, the Cups, the Swords, and the Skeleton who smiled at her.

"Don't bother me with such questions," she said. "I'm an old woman, which is already no joke. Why do you want to deprive me of the illusion that I was once the equal of a young man?"

"So you had the idea, when you left the old Turk, that you stopped being a woman?"

"For heaven's sake, no! How mixed up you are! We never have to stop being a woman. Not on any account, my girl. And even—get this into your head—a couple of women can live together a long time and be happy. But if one of the two women lets herself behave in the slightest like what I call a pseudo-man, then ..."

"Then the couple become unhappy?"

"Not necessarily unhappy, but sad."

"Oh? Explain, please."

Amalia laid out cabalistically her precious tarot cards, which smelled of greasy cardboard, old leather, and the tallow candles wine-cellar inspectors carry rolled up in a worn-out old bag.

"You see, when a woman remains a woman, she is a complete human being. She lacks nothing, even insofar as her *amie* is concerned. But if she ever gets it into her head to try to be a man, then she's grotesque. What is more ridiculous, what is sadder, than a woman pretending to be a man? On that subject, you'll never get me to change my mind. La Lucienne, from the time she adopted men's clothes, well!... Do you imagine her life wasn't poisoned from then on?"

"Poisoned by what?"

"From that time on, my pet, if her lady friends sometimes forgot that she wasn't a man, she, for her part, the little fool, never stopped thinking about it... And so, despite all her successes, she never stopped being resentful. That obsession deprived her of sleep and of faith in herself, which is even worse. Oh, she was a good sport, yes. But a discontented one. Mind you, I say discontented, not sad. A little sadness doesn't hurt a ménage of two women. Sadness, you might say, fills the void. Find a woman who hasn't felt wistful over a period in her life when she was sad!"

"It fills the void"—the remark smacks of unisexuality. It develops from the strict seclusion in which a feminine passion is confined, that period of sensual instruction, that rigorous induction without which, declared the Duc de Morny, a woman remains an unfinished sketch* This enlightened amateur in such matters elaborates his theory to

* *Journal des Goncourt.*

[107]

such an extent that, if I remember correctly, we understand he is not merely thinking of a "diploma in sensuality" but seems to consider—since diamond polishes diamond—that a woman refines a woman, leaves her softened, more pliable, one might still better say, bruised. Morny evidently spoke as an experienced man who would seek out a woman for a daring collaboration: "I hand over to you an incomplete marvel . . . . See that you perfect her and hand her back to me!"

"It was then," Amalia went on, "that La Lucienne began to make trouble. She began to adopt all the mean ways of love: there were affairs broken off without reason, there were reconciliations, but conditional, and separations, and unnecessary flights, tearful scenes, and I don't know what all . . . An obsession . . . Loulou, a pretty blonde she had with her, well, she threw her out one night half naked into the garden to teach her a lesson and make her decide what she wanted, that is, to choose between her, Lucienne, and Loulou's husband. Before dawn, Lucienne leaned out over the balcony: 'Have you thought it over?' she says. 'Yes,' says the girl, who was sniffling with the cold. 'Well?' says Lucienne. 'Well,' says the girl, 'I'm going back to Hector. I've just realized he can do something you can't.' 'Oh, naturally!' says Lucienne, spitefully. 'No,' says Loulou, 'it's not what you think, I'm not all that crazy about you know what. But I'm going to tell you something. When you and I go out together, everyone takes you for a man, that's understood. But for my part, I feel humiliated to be with a man who can't do *pipi* against a wall.'"

[108]

At the end of this story, Amalia commented: "Did you ever? Lucienne expected almost anything but that. She took it bad. So bad that she never saw Loulou again. Why are you laughing?"

"My goodness, at what Loulou said. It's childish!"

Amalia levelled on me her wrathful big eyes.

"Childish! Why, my pet, Loulou simply found the unkindest thing in the world to say!"

"I don't see why. To me, her retort was childish, rather comic."

"The unkindest thing in the world, I repeat! Such things can't be explained. There are ... subtleties ... you have to feel them. If you don't understand, then I can't explain it to you. And I really wonder what interests you in these subjects which you don't at all understand! Let me be, now. You've upset me enough in my 'fate'!"

She lowered her long lashes on her withered cheeks and remained severely silent as she read her fortune, moving a gouty index finger over the cards ...

How many times did I not "upset her in her 'fate' "? I pretended to be naïve to hear her talk. I loved to search her face, studying the thick eyebrows and the Roman chin for traces of that warrior girl who at night hurried through the alleyways of the Orient, passed through and outdistanced a number of dangers, and, on a body exactly like her own, as if fondly patterned on her own, tightened her arms ... Her arms, the final beauty, polished, greenish-white as are the arms of Tunisian Jewesses, and robust ... arms that had cradled the confident slumbers of

[109]

young women and shimmered through the veiling tresses of long hair.

"Listen, Amalia, see here ... Why do you suppose Loulou chose to go back to her husband? How do you explain it?"

"I have nothing to explain," said Amalia stiffly. "Besides, I never said she did go back."

"What was her husband like?"

"Very good-looking," said Amalia with sudden keen sympathy. "A handsome, fair-haired lad, golden-blond, oh yes, my goodness, one of those big peaceable fellows ... And no trouble at all to Loulou. In fact, rather too peaceable ..."

She raised her eyes, focusing them on the golden-haired young man in the far recesses of her memory, then again made her hostile estimate: "Yes, rather shifty. But very, very patient. The patience of an angel!"

Very patient ... "See that you perfect her and hand her back to me!" As for perfecting her, well and good, but hand her back? When I recall my conversations with Amalia, I feel that masculine imprudence in such a case is great. Supposing the precious hostage, summoned to return to the straight and narrow, told her lover, "No, I'm not coming back to you, I'm better off here than across the street"?

"The important thing, for Loulou, you see, was to revenge herself with a terrible word, to hurt Lucienne."

"Hurt Lucienne! A terrible word? You make me laugh, you sound like a schoolgirl. Such childish goings on! The big peaceable fellow must have laughed harder than I. He was biding his time."

"Childish goings on? How crass you are! How dare you talk like that?"

She surveyed me contemptuously, flaring her nostrils, and her irritation exaggerated the majesty of her features, making them look as if but a mask over that hidden face that spoils the looks of some women, the face of a bad priest, a face which seems to denounce their secret sins. This woman, well past sixty, still stood her ground against her triumphant rival and disputed his advantage with an impatience that imitated the chronically sulky face of Lucienne. Yes, well and good as for perfecting the girl, but as for handing her back . . .

I find it interesting to compare this tartness with the libertine calm of the man who resigns himself, a mocking spectator, to wait for the woman who for a time escapes him, as if to say, "Oh you, I'll nab you once more!" Such arrogance and such confidence deserve to be rewarded, as in fact they nearly always are.

"Amalia, were you faithful?"

"To whom?" said she, sarcastically.

"To your little friend?"

She affected a sudden disdain and raffishness.

"Oh! To women? It depends."

"Depends on what?"

"On the life we led together. If our work did not allow us to live together, my little friend and I, then I wasn't faithful. And neither was she."

"Why?"

I remember that once more Amalia wearily shrugged, raising her vast shoulders weighed down by the disastrous bulk of the breasts which pulled them forward.

"That's the way it is. What do you expect me to say? It's necessary to have gone through it. And me, I did go through it. That's the way it is. A woman isn't faithful to a woman who isn't there."

At this point I did not torment her further, for I felt sure she would never go beyond that boastful, "Me, I went through it."

I liked to touch the absolute limits of her ignorance and her sapience. About two kinds of loves she knew as much as can be learned from experience and a realistic hardihood. The wellspring of her memories having run dry, along with her blustering good humour, I left her to her "Knave of swords" and, without her, I pursued the subject further.

# SEVEN

How RELUCTANT I AM to handle dispassionately anything in creation as perilously fragile as an amorous
ménage of two women! The time is past when I could be
emotionally affected, but I still retain the necessary im-
partiality, the delicate point of view on what is really
delicate and poignant—the attempt at a union of two such
creatures, almost invariably well-meaning at first . . . In
their exalted state they forgot that they are being swayed
by the nest-building instinct of industrious females, destined to found and fill a home, as they assemble the
materials for constructing a sentimental refuge: the roof
unstable and immaterial, shored up by apposed foreheads,
clasped hands, united lips . . . Yes, I want to speak with
dignity, that is, with warmth, of what I call the noble
season of feminine passion. I write "noble season" and
not "season of noble love", for even if it has lost its purity
I can only compare it to the burningly passionate and
chaste season of betrothals.

The noble season of love, condemned by most people,
shows its nobility by disdaining unambiguous sensual
pleasure, by refusing to reflect, to see things clearly, and to
plan a future. When could they lay hold of a sense of the

future, those two enamoured women who, at every moment, demolish and deny it, who envisage neither beginning nor end nor change nor solitude, who breathe the air only *à deux*, and, arm in arm, walk only in perfect step with each other? It is the period when a monstrous life is established, set up like a contemplation in front of a mirror, a life whose regularity would stifle normal love. The woman who has given herself to a man is beloved, is demanding, but even at the height of her happiness she can never banish the intermittent idea of eventual loneliness: "Some day when *he* has gone . . . On that bench I shall wait for *him* . . ." Indeed, every time she rejects her lover, is she not extending the dangers that threaten the human couple? But it is otherwise when the couple is formed apart from a man. Two women immersed in each other do not fear, can no longer imagine a separation that would be intolerable. The pudicity that separates two lovers during the hours of repose, of ablutions, of illness never insinuates itself between two twin bodies that have similar afflictions, are subject to the same cares, the same predictable periods of chastity . . . A woman marvels at herself, is thrilled by her resemblance to the woman she loves and pities . . . Miracles of weakness and of timid attainments! In living amorously together, two women may eventually discover that their mutual attraction is not basically sensual—in contradiction to the cynical opinions expressed by Renée Vivien. Oh, the pathetically infantile and distraught cynicism of Renée! What woman would not blush to seek out her *amie* only for sensual pleasure? In no way is it passion that fosters the devotion of two women, but rather a feeling of kinship. "O my sisters!" Renée Vivien was constantly sighing. But in her verse she constantly pictures her sisters as being more or less languishing, torn with anguish, soaked in salt tears. I have written "kinship" when perhaps I should have used the word "similarities". The close resemblance even sets at ease sensual desire. A woman finds pleasure in caressing a body whose secrets she knows, her own body giving her the clue to its preferences.

"Oh, poor little thing!" What a sweet cry, full of pride and compassion! Thus a woman lamented and cradled the woman she loved, whom she had just helped to reach the peak of felicity ... Then she abandoned her to silence, never obliging her to utter those words that fan the faintly glowing embers but disrupt the delicate solidarity that is maintained only by incessant and united efforts. If, parted, the two shadows, replicas of each other—like the shadows of two balustrades, slender here, swollen there—allow an intruder to enter the space between them, it is enough to ruin the well-constructed edifice.

And the shadow projected on the intervening space need not be that worst intruder, a man. The most ordinary irruption can mortally change the steady hothouse warmth in which two women devote themselves to the cultivation of a delusion. Often it is a man who appears, faithful to his mission of enchanting and exhausting women merely by his dazzling difference. By contrast, he seems the very embodiment of luxury and ostentation. He is as necessary and steadfast as a rigorous natural climate, but he likes to be desired as a superfluity. Occasionally the female couple have time to block up the route by which he penetrated, and heroically they again live united, having shared everything, even the supreme deprivation.

Some will say that I give the smallest role to the feverish pleasure of the senses, in this chapter where women pass and pass again, two by two. The reason for this is my conviction that Sapphic libertinage is the only unacceptable one.

We can never sufficiently blame the Sapphos met by chance in restaurants, in dance halls, on the Blue Train, on the sidewalk, those provocative women who laugh but cannot sigh. We can never bring enough twilight, silence, and gravity to surround the embrace of two women. And so I managed to keep my good humour when recalling, when relating certain licentious traits of that good soul, Amalia, who sinned through gaiety when she recounted her "bachelor's life". Two women very much in love do not shun the ecstasy of the senses, nor do they shun a sensuality less concentrated than the orgasm, and more warming. It is this unresolved and undemanding sensuality that finds happiness in an exchange of glances, an arm laid on a shoulder, and is thrilled by the odour of sun-warmed wheat caught in a head of hair. These are the delights of a constant companionship and shared habits that engender and excuse fidelity. How marvellously compact, the repetition of days, repeated like the reflections of a lamp in a perspective of mirrors! Perhaps this love, which according to some people is outrageous, escapes the changing seasons and the wanings of love by being controlled with invisible severity, nourished on very

[116]

little, permitted to live gropingly and without a goal, its unique flower being a mutual trust such as that other love can never plumb or comprehend, but only envy; and so great is such a love that by its grace a half century can pass by like "a day of delicious and exquisite retirement".

I have copied those last words, fallen a hundred times from the pen of Lady Eleanor Butler and a hundred times stowed away like a sentimental bookmark, between the pages of her Journal.*

In May 1778, two wellborn young girls, related to the Welsh aristocracy, ran away together and, having chosen their fate, cloistered their solitude, their reciprocal tenderness for fifty-three years, in Llangollen, a small town in Wales. Lady Eleanor Butler, the elder of the two, died at the age of ninety. In 1825 Sir Walter Scott paid a visit to the women, who were by that time known as "the Ladies of Llangollen", and his son-in-law took it upon himself to tell us that they were "ridiculous". But in 1828 Prince Pückler-Muskau, while agreeing that their old-fashioned clothes did make them look "somewhat ludicrous", insisted that both ladies were characterized by

* This diary reads, on the title page, "Journal of E.B. and S.P. Inhabitants of a Cottage in the Vale of Llangollen, N. Wales. Written by E.B." It is the key document in *The Hamwood Papers*, ed. by G. H. Bell (John Travers), Macmillan and Co., Ltd., 1930. Where possible, we are quoting directly from these sources, rather than doing a re-translation of Colette's French version, while following Colette's plan, which was to omit dates and not even keep to the chronology. At one point in this chapter Colette writes, "I translate here and there, I reverse the order, and I do not excuse myself at all!"—*Translator's note*.

"that agreeable *aisance*, that air of the world of the *ancien régime*" which counteracted this; moreover, they were "courteous . . . without the slightest affectation, speaking French well," and above all they were endowed with "that essentially polite, unconstrained, and simply cheerful manner of the grand society of that day . . ."

I have only one picture of them: a reproduction of a mediocre portrait painted towards the end of their lives. Lady Eleanor seems to be the smaller of the two. Facing the spectator, she is stiffly encased in a black garment of heavy material, with a tight little spencer, a voluminous skirt, the cut of the outfit bespeaking the village dressmaker. Under two superimposed skirts, gathered up by the left hand of the sitter, can be glimpsed a little white petticoat and square-toed low-heeled slippers. The withered throat is concealed by an ascot neck scarf. The outfit of Miss Sarah Ponsonby is identical to that of Lady Eleanor, and the same important top hat, a kind of coal scuttle with curved brim, is worn by the two friends. The ensemble does not abstain from including the inevitable accessories of the period—rocky landscape, fountain shaped like a baptismal font, Gothic arches, and white wolfhound playfully standing on its fragile hind legs.

I would like to have known the faces of these two opinionated ladies as they were when young and radiant with mutual trust. But all I have in my hands is the account of their life, which I have read slowly and not without some difficulty in the original text.

Their flight was a great scandal, but once curiosity was exhausted, tokens of friendship and esteem came from all

parts to "the Ladies of Llangollen", and *visites distinguées*
—Lady Eleanor employs the French words—were never
lacking. Mme de Genlis reports that "both ladies have
the noblest manners and highly cultivated minds", but
after this beginning she falls into respectable bewilder-
ment mingled with pity for those "imprudent victims of
the most dangerous exaltation of the mind and heart"
who, in that excited state, had exchanged vows that left
them "forever chained to their mountain . . . In the eyes
of the world, the fate of a Carmelite must surely be less
pitiable!"

Leaving Mme de Genlis to the "torrents of tears" expected in the literature of that time, I am inclined to put
more faith in Prince Pückler-Muskau, who writes: "Nothing beyond their cottage interests the venerable ladies. It is
true, their dwelling contains some veritable treasures: a
well-stocked library, a delightful site and view . . . A calm
and peaceful life, a perfect friendship . . . such are their
blessings . . ."

They were glad to die "respected". That is a weakness
old age rarely escapes—one must also consider that they
were both extremely well born and well bred.

At the source of their serenity, going back a half century, they at least could find, still warm in its ashes, the
romantic memory of their first elopement, the wild race
at night on foot through mountainous roads, their feet
bleeding in fragile cloth slippers . . . They could remember
two nights out in the open, sleeping in a ruined barn,
Sarah shivering with cold in spite of the protective arms
around her—nights of anxiety, of mounting fever, and

[119]

then the approach of the pursuers guided by the barking of Sarah's little dog.

Infatuated with romance, they had leaped from a window rather than leave by way of the open door. They corresponded with each other by secret means, bribed the servants, and, at the moment of leaving, had seized firearms they did not know how to use and fled on horseback, although they had never in their lives sat a horse . . . There were complications, legal processes, tragedies, childish tears . . . but from all this a unique sentiment sprang, straight and firm and flowering like the iris nestling against its green stem.

The younger of the fugitives, Sarah Ponsonby, when caught and taken back home after their first flight, almost died of pneumonia as a result of it. In her feverish delirium she kept repeating her firm intention of dying, leaving off only to call out for her friend Eleanor. And that friend "of robust character" neither wept nor screamed but escaped from her home at night and rejoined the moribund Sarah, hiding herself and living in a cupboard.

In short, what did they want? Almost nothing. Everything. They wanted to live together. When at last the two families yielded, overwhelmed, unable to make "head or tail" of this folly, of this pure but irregular passion, the two girls suddenly became as gentle as tame doves. In the bosom of the conquered and tearful Ponsonby family, they serenely and with angelic cruelty organized their final departure. "They dined with us," writes a Mrs Goddard in her diary, "and I have never seen anything so confident as their behaviour ... At six in the morning they set out as merry as possible."

From that day onward, the matter was settled. A vow of reclusion descended on this couple of young girls, separating them from the world, veiling and changing and remaking the universe in their eyes. In the distance would rumble and then die down the storm of no-popery riots in London; the United States would proclaim its independence; a queen and king of France would perish on the scaffold; Ireland would revolt, the British fleet would mutiny; slavery would be abolished ... The universal excitement, the conflagration of Europe did not cross the Pengwern Hills that shut in Llangollen, or disturb the waters of the little river Dee. We would know nothing more of "the Ladies of Llangollen" had not the elder, according to the fashion of the time, kept a diary, only twice interrupted in forty-three years. As usual with perfectly happy people, the younger woman neglected all means of expression and, mute, became a sweet shadow. She was no longer Sarah Ponsonby, but a part of that double person called "we". She even lost her name, which Lady Eleanor almost never mentioned in the diary. From then on she was called "Beloved" and "Better Half" and "Delight of my Heart".

Now let us enter, full of awe, the fantastic atmosphere, let us shatter the imaginary barrier, let us tread the meadows where the turf is as buoyant as a cloud and as green as the green in our dreams, grazed by a "silver and purple ray" coming from no one knows where, laminated between two mountains ...

*Read Madame de Sévigné. My Love drawing. From seven till nine in sweet converse with the delight of my heart, over the Fire. Paper'd our Hair.*

*Incessant rain the entire evening. Shut the shutters, made a good fire, lighted the Candles . . . A day of strict retirement, sentiment, and delight.*

*From seven till ten I read Rousseau. A day of Peace and delight. Felt and enjoy'd our retirement.*

*A day of the most perfect and sweet retirement.*

*Rose at seven. A sweet spring morning . . . Ten. My beloved and I drank a dish of tea . . . A day of most delicious and exquisite retirement.*

*My beloved and I went the Home Circuit . . . Soft fine rain. Began Les Mémoires de Madame de Maintenon. I doubt whether the Vulgarity of style, absurd anecdotes, and impertinent reflections will permit me to read it.*

*Writing, Drawing, sweet sunshine, blue sky. Soft smoke from the village ascending in spirals . . . Birds innumerable.*

*My beloved and I went a delicious walk round Edward Evans' field . . .*

I cannot help but stop to read again and again that

[122]

phrase which commemorates one day among many: *My beloved and I went a delicious walk* ... Had she been less simple and thought more about what would become of her diary after her death, would Lady Eleanor have stopped there? To dazzle posterity and confound their detractors it would suffice for the two friends to have left on one of those sheets of paper used by Sarah for her paintings of birds and flowers merely that sentence which tells the whole story of their life together: *My beloved and I went a delicious walk* ...

They "went the Home Circuit" and went on delicious walks together for fifty-one years. During the first years of that charming stroll, did they wear the white frocks that were in the English fashion, with a fichu crossed over the bosom and loosely knotted beneath it? These daughters of Quality serenely lacked money: *My Heart's darling and I ... sat by the Kitchen Fire, talking of our Poverty.* I would be willing to swear that they talked about their poverty as if it were one more blessing, exclusive, and captured within their fenced enclosure: our poverty, our gooseberries, our darling cow Margaret, our shoes that we are going to break in, our hair that the hairdresser must arrange ...

If Eleanor Butler did not write "our tomb", it was, no doubt, because she shrank from those words which touched upon the extreme intimacy of their ultimate couch. But she never tired of making veiled allusions to it:

*A day of delicious retirement. In the evening my beloved and I wrote and signed a Paper. Sealed it*

*with three Black Seals and deposited it in the upper*
*flat Drawer of the Desk. There to remain till after*
*our Decease when we trust the request contained in it*
*will be accorded.*

Had she not mentioned the three black seals, we would
have invented them, demanded them. Three blobs of
black sealing wax, the winter night, a solemn oath, and
the two names affixed beneath the oath ... We smile.
Such childish performances are common to so many passionate loves! What is uncommon in so many passionate
loves is to endure half a century, without change or varia-
tion. Having said, written, signed, exchanged some whispered words, listened to the December wind, the twelve
strokes of midnight, the owls, and having summoned all
the ghosts inhabiting a Welsh cottage, the two friends
lighted a lantern and went out, hand in hand, to the
stables to pay a call on "darling Margaret", the cow.

Beyond time, beyond reach ... Now and then they
briefly felt the shock of reality. Their flight was much
talked about and the newspapers sometimes recalled it.
Lady Eleanor then took offence, wrote to influential
friends, complained to her distinguished kinsmen. What
did the blissful and mute Sarah Ponsonby think about all
this? We shall never know. The diary informs us that on
the day in 1789 when the Comte de Jarnac visited the two
friends and told about the events in Paris—the flight of
Louis XVI to Versailles, his return, the rioting in the
streets, various horrors—the Well-Beloved was finishing a
letter pouch in white satin with gold initials bordered in

shaded blue and gold, lock-stitched in white silk, the whole thing hemmed in pale blue. And Lady Eleanor adds, "The Comte de Jarnac . . . went away and left us charmed with him." She does not disdain to set down in her precise and cold English manner a summary of the revolutionary days, but she immediately returns to more important things.

> *My Beloved and I walked to Blaen Bache . . . Found a very pretty young woman spinning . . . a little child with a Doll, two fine dogs . . . a black and white cat . . .*

Infantile adventures, fairylands of love—and much that she dared not say. A touch of human respect prevents her from adding, "a fairy sitting in a clump of bindweed, a little man with bird-feet . . . and a booted squirrel." No, she relates only what ordinary mortals can believe.

> *My beloved and I gathered holly berries, primrose and strawberry plants for our Banks . . . Then visited a cow, saw her suckling her son . . . went to the new garden, gathered gooseberries . . .*

The fantastic tale cares not a whit for the equinoxes! The elastic turf, greener than green, can next day be covered with a crystal powdering of frost. Above the cottage and its hill, did there even exist a season of fine weather or a season of bad weather? No. There was only Llangollen weather.

[125]

*Soft fine rain. My Beloved and I went the Home Circuit. Celestial lovely day.*

The magic of this radiant friendship reduced the Welsh villagers to a state of adoration, and also seemed to affect the very animals, which became spellbound in the vicinity of the cottage.

*A Rabbit in the Shrubbery. Sent to the village for hounds to hunt it. No Noses. Nor indeed Eyes. Could neither smell nor see the Rabbit which sat before them by the Library window.*

United for better or worse, they disdained nothing. Their beautiful hands unlinked to do housework, scatter seeds in the kitchen garden, oil the furniture, polish each marvel of their blessed and restricted universe.

*Rose at six . . . My Beloved and I went to the garden . . . Sowed three sorts of cucumber seeds . . . Oiled the Parlour eating table with the Spinhamland receipt. Dined in the kitchen to let the oil sink in it . . . dined very comfortably on lamb and cold mutton . . . Found Margaret* [the cow] *at the gate waiting for admittance. Opened it for her. Walked round our little demesne, returned home by the lane . . . The country in a blaze of beauty.*

Intentionally I neglect all the dates of this Journal. Lady Eleanor noted them with care, no doubt fearing that the fugitive gold, the immateral dust of time would come all too quickly to dry the ink . . .

I do not mention the numerous revealing traits that slipped from the pen of the provincial aristocrat which Lady Eleanor Butler was, genial with the villagers of Llangollen but ready to "refuse with proper contempt" any "Creatures without names and certainly without manners" who try to pass through the white gate. Although she was infatuated with genealogy and proud in later life that the "bon ton" came to visit her and her amorous shadow, she saw to it that the visitors did not stay too long. Moreover, the cottage was relatively small. Lady Eleanor does not detail, in the Journal, the arrangement of the room she admires more each day (*I am so sure it is like Madame de Sévigné's cabinet*), and if I mistake not, the words "the bedroom" and "our bed" occur but once. English readers, more strait-laced and more perverted than I, are free to see in this a proof . . . but a proof of what?

Envious of a devotion as tranquil as this, some would have it that these two faithful spinsters fell short of purity —but what do they mean by purity? I pick a quarrel with those who consider that patting a young cheek, fresh and warm and velvety as a peach, does not violate the proprieties but that caressing and lightly weighing with the cupped hand a rosy breast shaped like a peach is a cause for blushes, alarmed cries, slurs cast upon the character of the assailant . . . How hard it is for respectable people to believe in innocence! Oh, I know, I know quite well that the cheek remains cool, while the breast becomes excited.

[127]

Well, so much the worse for the breast! O indiscreet little breast, can you not allow us to hover over you, selfishly meditating and calling up visions of pulpy fruit, rosy dawns, snowy landscapes? Can you not allow us to wander among the planets or simply think of nothing? Why are you not like warm marble, impersonal, law-abiding, and respectful of the caressing hand? We do not ask your opinion, but there you are, at once devoid of mystery, imploring, and shamefully virile ... "In cases of public morals," an old judge once said, "it is almost always the victim who is guilty ..."

The bedroom ... our bed ... What I would like to have is the diary that would reveal the victim, the diary that the younger of this couple, Sarah Ponsonby, might have kept. Eleanor, who speaks for both and wields the pen, has nothing to hide from us. The secret here is Sarah, who says nothing, and embroiders. What a light would be shed by a diary she kept; surely she would have confessed everything; now and then there would be the hint of a subtle and perhaps traitorous attraction, a wealth of sensual effusions. See here, stout-hearted Eleanor, you who were responsible for all the daily decisions, you who were so profoundly submerged in your Well-Beloved, were you unaware that two women cannot achieve a perfect union? You were the prudent warden—the masculine element. It was you who measured the distance at which the real world must be kept, who gave to some parts of a few miles of rolling countryside a pastoral aspect. Your urbanity, which opened wide the cottage door to the well-born passer-by, knew still better how to shut it. Promptly your modest turnout was harnessed and you drove, you and your Well-Beloved, towards villages, towards friendly neighbours, towards certain vistas. The same carriage brought you back the same evening, and on your return journey you had with you the full moon, the odour of new-mown hay, the hooting of the wood owl ... And every midnight for fifty years and more found you and your beloved reunited under the roof tiles. And one night: "... We found on our bed, in the bedroom, the Christmas gifts that our best friends and servitors ..."

Here the ordinary reader smiles. Nor does he forgo a sniff of amused superiority. But I am not an ordinary reader. I do not smile at this hour closed in upon two women who, refusing to be the parody of a couple, pass through, leave out the stage of spurious nuptials and attain the refuge of sleeping together, lying awake together, experiencing together nocturnal terrors ... The weaker one tightens her arms round the neck of the elder one, breathes in the odour of her thick hair, grits her teeth, permits herself neither to sob nor to whimper: "How far we are from everyone! How alone we are ..." And the older woman, menaced by no peril, lays a protective arm around her friend's shoulder and in the darkness clenches her free fist: "If anyone dared to come here to take her away from me, I'd ..." And in the darkness she listens to her own accelerated heartbeat, for two women who have resolved to live alone together are never safe. Everything is permitted them except one kind of quietude.

And that is why I contemplate, with a friendly and comprehending emotion, the bedroom invaded by fear and at last visited by sleep and finally by the dawn—*the* bedroom and *the* bed where repose two sweet, foolish creatures, so intensely loyal to a delusion.

Love, housework, gardening; in the evening, reading; visits received and paid back; long, worldly and detailed correspondence; English gormandizing—cold mutton being favoured equally with "the fruit of the Passiflora served with sugar and Madeira wine"—and how time flies! What, has it already been twenty years, already forty years that we are together? Why, how terrible! We haven't yet said all we wanted to say to each other . . . May we have a little respite, or else may we be allowed to begin all over again! And "Oh!" says Lady Eleanor to herself, trembling, for she will soon be eighty. "Oh, that poor little thing, the Delight of my Heart, that little one I shall leave all alone . . . Why, it was only yesterday, only this morning that I noted in my Journal her touching way of giving me my emetic, anxiously, with that goodness that is the joy of my life . . . Oh, that dear child, my Better Half, who is only sixty-six and knows nothing of life . . ."

It was about this period that the commonplace portrait I'm so fond of was painted, the portrait of two old spinsters in riding habits . . . And the moment comes, not long afterwards, when Lady Eleanor Butler dies, at the age of ninety.

The friend she forsook waited only two years to rejoin her in the bed made up in advance in the narrow room provided for under the secret of the three black beeswax seals. And at this point, my confidence in the silent embroiderer is restored, for although *The Hamwood Papers* make much of a letter the Duke of Wellington wrote to the one remaining lady, no letter of Sarah Ponsonby bewails her loneliness and grief, and nowhere does she describe the death of Eleanor Butler or eulogize the character of the departed. Alone, bereaved, she shows herself worthy of her youthful self, that proud and impassioned girl who at twenty resolved to die. Just as a derelict clinging to a spar from the shipwreck does not dream of counting the blessings he has lost, Sarah Ponsonby did not dream of mourning aloud her lost friend. Her memorialist gives us only a short and final letter, completely to my taste, which does not depart from her passionate silence but disguises it beneath the musings of a girl no longer young:

*... A friend brought me 16 geraniums, 14 of which are perfectly new to me though already possessed of I think, four-score varieties. I will send you a list of them, for though Infants at present they may be parents in Spring and, some at least, be acceptable additions to yours in their Descendants at that Season. I am very much obliged for the Heartsease seed. I am afraid it will be of very difficult cultivation in these unfavourable times ...*

# EIGHT

EIGHTEEN HUNDRED AND THIRTY-ONE... Exactly a century has passed since the death of that survivor. Can we possibly, without apprehension, imagine two Ladies of Llangollen in this year of 1930? They would own a car, wear dungarees, smoke cigarettes, have short hair, and there would be a bar in their apartment. Would Sarah Ponsonby still know how to remain silent? Perhaps, with the aid of crossword puzzles. Eleanor Butler would curse as she jacked up the car, and would have her breasts amputated. No longer would there be a village blacksmith with whom she would have cordial relations; she would exchange familiar remarks with the garage man. And already, twenty years earlier, Marcel Proust had endowed her with shocking desires, customs, and language, thus showing how little he knew her.

Ever since Proust shed light on Sodom, we have had a feeling of respect for what he wrote, and would never dare, after him, to touch the subject of these hounded creatures, who are careful to blur their tracks and to propagate at every step their personal cloud, like the cuttlefish.

But—was he misled, or was he ignorant?—when he

assembles a Gomorrah of inscrutable and depraved young girls, when he denounces an entente, a collectivity, a frenzy of bad angels, we are only diverted, indulgent, and a little bored, having lost the support of the dazzling light of truth that guides us through Sodom. This is because, with all due deference to the imagination or the error of Marcel Proust, there is no such thing as Gomorrah. Puberty, boarding school, solitude, prisons, aberrations, snobbishness—they are all seedbeds, but too shallow to engender and sustain a vice that could attract a great number or become an established thing that would gain the indispensable solidarity of its votaries. Intact, enormous, eternal, Sodom looks down from its heights upon its puny counterfeit.

Intact, enormous, eternal. Those are big words which imply consideration, at least the consideration one owes to power. I don't deny it. Women are little acquainted—it goes without saying—with homosexuality, but when they encounter it, they adopt the attitude imposed by woman's instinct. Thus, facing the enemy, the rose beetle falls and plays dead; the great crab, immobile, arches its pincers; the grey tarente lizard clings, flattened, to the grey wall. We should not be expected to do more than we can.

A woman whom a man betrays for another man knows that all is lost. Containing her cries, her tears, her threats, which comprise the main part of her forces in an ordinary case, she does not struggle, but digs in or says nothing, fulminates scarcely at all, occasionally tries to find the way to an unrealizable alliance with the enemy, with a sin that dates as far back as the human race, a sin she neither

[133]

invented nor approved. She is far from adopting the mockingly licentious attitude of the man whose wife or mistress forsakes him for another woman: "Oh you, I'll get you back." Disillusioned, she renounces with bitter hatred and carefully conceals her great uncertainty, wondering, "Was he really destined for me?" For she has more humility than is generally believed. But since her subtlety is limited in range and since she judges severely the inclinations of the mind, she can never manage to separate the mental from the physical and stubbornly confuses "homosexual" with "effeminate men".

In a certain period of my youth, I associated for some time with various homosexuals, thanks to one of Monsieur Willy's ghost-secretaries. I am recalling now an epoch when I lived in a singular state of neglect and concealed wretchedness. Still very provincial—isn't it so, dear Jacques-Émile Blanche?—physically unsociable to the point of sometimes avoiding shaking hands or not letting my hand be kissed, I resented being isolated and forgotten in the gloomy flat as much as I resented being forced to appear in society. I therefore took great pleasure in the companionship of the secretary, like me a "ghost". He was young, wellborn, cheerful, impish, and he made no secret of his homosexual inclinations. He and I worked—the expression will still make a few of our colleagues smile, among others Pierre Veber, Vuillermoz, and Curnonsky—in the same "writers' workshop".

He confided in me and brought his friends to see me. With them I felt younger, I recovered my actual age. I laughed, reassured in the presence of so many inoffensive

young men. I learned how a well-dressed man dresses—
for they were for the most part English and had strict ideas
of elegance, and the same young fellow who secretly wore
next to his skin a turquoise cross on a neck chain would
never have allowed himself unconventional ties or hand-
kerchiefs.

Two rooms had been set aside for me in the conjugal
apartment, a bedroom and a studio, which I referred to
proudly as my "bachelor digs". In that studio, which was
equipped with a trapeze, there was as much laughter as in
a boarding school, exaggerated and youthful laughter.
But what strange talk went on there between gentlemen!

"What's happened, my dear fellow, to your young
boxer?"

"Boxer? I don't have a boxer!"

"I mean, that youngster who made cardboard boxes for
milliners and perfumers."

"Oh, that one! I have a poor memory. You should ask
me about a certain fireman of the city of Paris!"

"A fireman? How frightful!"

As a visiting card is thrust out under an insult, an un-
mounted photograph was thrust beneath the nose of the
disdainful one.

"How frightful, really? Take a look! This may make
you change your mind. And please note the belt with the
arms of Paris on it . . ."

Internationally famous, well preserved, my old friend
C. de X, who has since died of old age and whose friendship, youthful spirit, and charming manners I still miss,
climbed the three flights of stairs not without difficulty.

A dyed, square-cut beard concealed, so he said, his "old codger's wattles". The stubborn effort to survive bedewed his temples with sweat, which he lightly dabbed with his handkerchief. I can still see the thinness of his hand, on which great veins stood out, the grey of his jacket, the blue-grey of his silk handkerchief, the blue-grey of his eyes that were already faded, and the fixed smile that widened his mouth ... That old man, who was ashamed of nothing, managed to shock no one.

"Ouf!" he sighed, as he sat down. "Oh, to be only sixty again!"

Jean Lorrain speaks of him somewhere in *Poussières de Paris*, referring to his exceptional good looks, something about "the best pair of shoulders of the century", if I'm not mistaken.

"Why are you so out of breath? Where have you come from?" asked a young man, insultingly.

"From my mother's," replied C., giving himself the pleasure of not telling a lie, for in fact he was a tender and respectful son and lived with his almost centenarian mother. He looked the young man up and down and made a stinging rejoinder: "She is the only companion I have, sir. Has someone been telling you I have another?"

While the young man was still trying to think of a retort or an excuse, C. burst into a short laugh, then turned toward me and added, "I have no other since the departure of a young friend, who is travelling."

"Ah, yes? Where is he going?"

"Who knows? He had certain troubles that made him decide to leave."

[136]

He heaved a deep sigh, took a swallow of weak tea, and once more the blue handkerchief came into play as he dabbed his mouth and temple.

"He's such a nice boy, but absent-minded," C. went on. "Just imagine! A lady invites him to her house for a cup of hot chocolate—he is attractive. He accepts the invitation—and has one of his weak moments. While talking with her, he happens to drop something, I don't know what, into her cup of chocolate. Anyway, the lady wakes up two days later and finds—deplorable coincidence!— that all her furniture has disappeared. She thought she was dreaming, the poor lady. But no sooner did she recover her senses than she lodged a complaint against my absent-minded friend. And so, not wanting to be mixed up in a complicated affair, he went away. May heaven return him to us!"

Giving me a wink of his alert little dark eye, my friend the ghost-secretary questioned C. in a tone of sincerity.

"Tell me, dear sir, isn't that absent-minded young man the same young man who is supposed to have strangled a Turkish-bath attendant?"

Straightening up with a proud jerk that was especially due to stiff muscles, the old man defended himself with a wave of his fine, wrinkled hand.

"Gossip, dear boy, gossip! I'm a wise man, I am never jealous of the past!"

Tartness, theatrical cynicism, affectation, nonsensical jesting comprised the tone prescribed by this type of visitor. Sometimes violence, masculine or morbid, let out its brief cry, injected its brief warmth. For instance, a

[137]

mere boy, issuing from the distant times when good and evil, mingled like two liqueurs, made one, gave an account of his last night at the Élysée Palace-Hôtel:

"He made me feel afraid, that big man, in his bedroom ... I opened the little knife, I put one arm over my eyes, and with my other hand holding the knife, I went like this at the fat man, into his stomach ... And I ran away quick!"

He was radiant with beauty, with roguishness, with a kind of incipient madness. His listeners were tactful and cautious. No one exclaimed. Only my friend C., after a moment, casually said, "What a child!" and then changed the subject.

Lacking grandeur and malice, C. resembled the Baron de Charlus only generically. But it is this powerful late-comer on the stage, Charlus, who seems to serve as model, for even those who preceded him regard themselves as weak descendants and pay homage. Courage, if we reduce the word to its most ordinary and military meaning, did permit C., as it permitted Charlus, to graze real dangers, sometimes to court them—with this difference, that C., very far from having the masochistic deviation of Charlus, wanted only the best and most available of what he liked best. "At heart. I'm a French milliner," he stated. At any rate, he did not regard at all highly these cosmopolitan youths, gossipy and grasping, who offended the ancestor with their irony and crude familiarity.

Often in their company, rarely questioning them and never indulging in persiflage with them, I reassured these men, of whom I would be the last to say they lacked virility. A human being with a man's face is virile by the very fact that he contracts a dangerous way of life and the certainty of an exceptional death. My strange friends discussed all sorts of things in my presence—violent deaths, inevitable blackmails, fleecings, shameful lawsuits, cravats, cuffed trousers, music, literature, dowries, marriages—avoiding no subject of conversation in front of me, and I still wonder why society regards this category of men as irresponsible.

They know precisely what they like and dislike. They are aware of the perils of their chosen way of life, know the bounds of their particular prejudices, and if they pay lip service to caution, they often forget it.

They allowed me to share with them their sudden outbursts of gaiety, so shrill and revealing. They appreciated my silence, for I was faithful to their concept of me as a nice piece of furniture and I listened to them as if I were an expert. They got used to me, without ever allowing me access to a real affection. No one excluded me—no one loved me. I owe a great deal to their cool friendship, to their fierce critical sense. They taught me not only that a man can be amorously satisfied with a man but that one sex can suppress, by forgetting it, the other sex. This I had not learned from the ladies in men's clothes, who were preoccupied with men, who were always, with suspect bitterness, finding fault with men. My strange homosexual friends did not talk about women, except distantly and condescendingly. "Very pretty, that white on white beading that Bady wears in the third act," they would say. Or: "Oh, really, those enormous hats of Lantelme,

[139]

I'm fed up with them! Why doesn't she parcel them out?"

Absent yet present, a translucent witness, I enjoyed an indefinable peace, accompanied by a kind of conspiratorial pride.

I heard on their lips the language of passion, of betrayal and jealousy, and sometimes of despair—languages with which I was all too familiar, I had heard them elsewhere and spoke them fluently to myself. But my brazen young men stripped the words and sentiments of their murderous force, played with weapons turned aside from me, for as yet I had neither the strength nor the desire to put myself in a safe place. The "Young Greek God" had nothing to fear from me, not even a kiss; "Namouna" and "Once More" babbled in their maternal tongues; Édouard de Max paid us a visit, escorted by adolescents, like a god escorted by nymphs. He flattered them with his eyes, scolded them with his voice; for them he was nothing but tutelary indifference, hauteur, melancholy, all singularly aloof. A tyro in the career of diplomacy had the unfortunate idea of bringing along with him one day his intimate friend, Bouboule, decked out in a dress of black Chantilly lace over pale blue silk, his face sulky beneath a wide lace hat, as uncouth as a country wench in need of a husband, his cheeks plump and fresh as nectarines—such freshness not surprising in a seventeen-year-old butcher boy. We were frozen with astonishment, and aware that he was meeting with no success, kicking the hem of his skirt with his enormous feet, he left us. He did not go far, apparently, for only a few days later he committed suicide—the unexplained and clumsy act of a big boy, uncertain and chagrined.

He shattered with a revolver bullet his pretty pouting mouth, his low forehead beneath kinky hair, his anxious and timid little bright blue eyes . . . My circle of friends did not even give him the briefest funeral oration. On the other hand, these same young men talked excitedly and endlessly about the murder, in London, of the painter Z. . . . They classified it as a great curiosity and studied it like men who, both innocent and expert, can easily decipher the cryptograms written with a knife point on a slashed throat or with spurs on bloodstained thighs.

One of these friends received a long letter from London which he brought and read aloud. We all listened, reread, and absorbed it with the delectation of young wild beasts tasting blood. I heard shrill cries, hoarse blasphemies in English, obscure predictions:

"You'll see, it's another stroke of those damned three-shilling prostitutes of the . . ." He named a regiment.

"They? You flatter them!"

"I know what I'm saying. They're capable of anything that will prove they can be real he-men."

It may surprise some people that I could secretly apply the name "oasis" or "island" to this shore approached only by men tarred by the same brush, who arrived like the survivors of a cataclysm. Variously marked, variously formed, they all came from afar, from the beginning of time. They had traversed unscathed every epoch, every reign, without perishing, like a dynasty sure of its everlastingness. Self-centred, blinded by their own brilliance, they have bequeathed to us only a one-sided and romanticized documentation. But, up to now, were they ever observed by any woman for the length of time they have been observed by me? Ordinarily a woman—and let's say, an ordinary woman—tries to entice a homosexual. Naturally, she fails. She then declares she "despises" him. Or else—and the case is not rare—she wins a physical victory, which gives her a cause for pride; she has achieved a kind of brilliant advantage over him, but futile and misleading, because she gives an exaggerated importance to external signs, if I dare say so. She is bound to be disillusioned afterward and will forever loudly lay claim to what she calls her due. And from this arises deep resentment. She, who easily renounces getting from a normal man the same "due", providing her renouncement remains a secret, will not relinquish her claims on a catch she made by chance and by mistake. Powerless to bring about a repetition of the initial victory through chance and mischance, she hounds him and wilfully sinks into an unheard-of amorous despair. I wrote about such a young woman in *L'Entrave*, calling her May and making her unrecognizable.

Jealously and suspiciously she prowled about her lover, subjecting him to such a close watch that I reproached her for it.

"Well, what about me?" May burst out. "Am I not patient, haven't I been patient for almost a year now? Do you think it's natural to be like Jean? A man who doesn't get drunk, doesn't make scenes, doesn't receive in the mail anything but bills and postal cards, doesn't

[142]

ever have a really good time, and is never in the dumps?"

Wrathfully she clenched her tiny fists and shook them threateningly at her invisible adversary, a cold, solidly built young man, rather common when he talked, irreproachable when he remained silent. Then she shot me a glance that sent me packing and returned to her quest, grumbling and whining. I must say that, with her snub nose, her wide-set, prominent, and glittering eyes, she resembled a blond bulldog. Although he was visibly bored, she kept dragging Jean back to the studio gymnasium.

"What can you see in that couple you first brought here?" I asked my friend, the ghost-secretary, referring to this couple.

"The man is amusing," he said vaguely, after letting his birdlike eyes, alert and black and inexpressive, linger first on them and then on me.

"Amusing!" I exclaimed. "The woman perhaps, that little clown without a nose. But the man?"

"I may be mistaken," said the ghost, with the punctilious politeness he knew how to make discomfiting.

But from then on I noticed that two people were spying upon May's lover: May and the ghost.

Insupportable chatterbox, but harmless and friendly, May chatted for the most part with the younger of the two Englishmen, the one who was called "Once More". Those two innocents recovered their childhood on the trapeze, hanging from the rings, improvising circus stunts, and Jean, all smooth surfaces, patient, uncommunicative, laughed at them rather grudgingly.

[143]

One evening, May and her gymnastic partner could be seen whispering and plotting together; then they disappeared and May came back, making a grand entrance, simpering, dressed in the navy-blue suit of "Once More", a scarf around her neck, the cap slanted over one eye.

"What about it, Jean?"

"Ravishing! Gaby Deslys as an Apache!" exclaimed the ghost.

"You think!" said May, annoyed. "Why, I'm completely 'Once More'! Deah me, fawncy seeing her heah!" she said, aping the young Englishman. "Can't you see, Jean?"

Wagging her hips, she approached her lover and pressed herself against him like a pet animal. I only saw that he bent his head toward her and that his mouth seemed suddenly to swell. May let out a strange little cry, the scream of a caught rabbit, retreated toward me, and Jean excused himself to me, repeating agitatedly, "I didn't do anything to her, I didn't do anything to her."

But he could still not control his expression, and his mouth was in fact swollen, his eyes pale, glaring with hatred at May, forbidding her to caricature a secret idol secretly revered ...

Then he controlled himself, and the face he had briefly exposed was soon again masked. May courageously tried to give another interpretation to the weird scream of a wounded rabbit she had uttered by repeating it intentionally, on a variety of notes. And still shrieking "Eee! Eee!" she left the room to put on her dress and her big plumed hat. When she reappeared, Jean stood up, ready to take her home. But she decided otherwise.

"No, no, go home on your own, just let me have the carriage, I want to go to the rue de Rivoli to pick up my fur-lined coat, it should be ready by now."

He went off obediently, as if walking in his sleep, and May, following him, gave me a shrewd and outraged look. But I had not the least desire to bring that poor girl to admit the existence of a category of man who craves men, who is reserved for men and is as noxious as the fruit of the tropical poison tree to any woman he happens to attract.

Despair born of frustration drove women, after the war, to imitate the looks and manners of androgynous young men. They had reckoned on their men being delivered back to them full of frenzied desire. Then, becoming aware that their own apotheosis was not very dazzling, they began wildly to imitate the outward looks of the male tribe that was causing them such heartache. They cropped their hair, squandered a fortune at the shirtmaker's, and drank to excess. And they gained no ground, for they were not disinterested enough.

Without meaning to, this behaviour of women contributed to the creation of a type of young man both effeminate and cruel, wearing ochre make-up, thinking only of getting ahead, no matter how. I find this type very different from my friends of 1898 and 1900 as I remember them. They may have been scandalous, but only moderately so, and fatuous, but their extravagance went no further than the moonstone and the chrysoprase. They were ridiculous,

[145]

certainly, but in those bygone times their behaviour did not completely disguise them; I could still recognize in them a primitive bloom, the strength of deceptively frail-looking people; I could still see in them the gravity and the savagery of love.

As I write these words, I am thinking of a couple who never mingled with my usual visitors ... But I am afraid that if I merely specify that the elder of the two was a scholar, a poet, a writer, beautiful from head to foot, he might be recognized ... As for his protégé, his skin reminded one of ripe wheat, of apple blossoms, and he had the dignity of a child of old peasant stock, as indeed he was; he spoke little and listened attentively to his tutor and friend. Together they lived a quiet life, outside Paris. I can still see the hostile glances they shot at my flamboyant coterie when they unexpectedly arrived one day.

"Sh..." whispered the elder, before he addressed me in a low voice. "Don't disturb these ... charming individuals. We've just dropped in to say *au revoir*—we're going away, tonight."

"Where are you going?"

"To Touraine, with the youngster, for the harvesting. They need his help."

"And you?"

"I too will help with the harvesting."

He thrust beneath my eyes his weathered hands, the hands of a great traveller, his wrists as hard as saplings.

"We're making the trip on foot," he added. "And not for the first time. It's so much more agreeable."

The "youngster", his impatient eyes a resplendent blue, was already waiting for the signal to depart, eager for the long march beneath the June night sky, the halts along the road and the vagabond meals, the warm bread bought in the villages on the way. Shorter than the elder man, upon whom he modelled himself admiringly, the boy carried himself easily, head high. What would time do to such an attachment?

The elder, killed in action during the war, was not among those who let themselves be forgotten. I will not bequeath his letters to anyone. I wonder about the younger one. When he stirs the windrows with the pitchfork, does he still feel a sinking of his heart that was once full to overflowing? Friendship, male friendship, unfathomable sentiment! Why should the sob of ecstasy be the one release denied you?

I am betraying a tolerance that some will condemn as strange. It is true that the association of the male couple I have just briefly sketched had, for me, the aspect of union and even of dignity. A kind of austerity overlaid it which I can compare to no other, for it held nothing of parade or precaution, nor did it spring from the morbid fear that galvanizes more often than it checks so many among those hounded by society. I find it in me to see in homosexuality a kind of legitimacy and to acknowledge its eternal character. I used to be archly scandalized that the male was attracted less, in the female form, to the charm of a deep snare, a smooth abyss, a living marine corolla, than to the occasional assertion of the woman's most virile characteristics—and I am not forgetting the breast. A man is attracted toward what can reassure him, to what he can recognize in that convex feminine body which is exactly the opposite of his own, disquieting, never familiar, with its ineradicable odour which is not even earthy but is borrowed from sea wrack, from the original slime . . .

Those who helped me at that time when my life was nothing but constraint and a lie imposed upon me made it clear that the antipathy of one sex for the other is not necessarily pathological. As I moved into other milieus, I noted that the viewpoint of "normal" people is not so very different. I have said that what I particularly liked in the world of my "monsters" where I moved in that distant time was the atmosphere that banished women, and I called it "pure". But, for that matter, I would have liked as well the purity of the desert, the purity of the prison. Prison and desert are not, however, within the reach of everyone.

Tenderly, then, I recall the monsters who accompanied me for a long way during that part of my life which was not easy. Monsters—that is a word soon said. So much for monsters. Why, as to those who diverted me from my troubles, I could name them thus and implore them from the depths of myself, "O monsters, do not leave me alone . . . I do not confide in you except to tell you about my fear of being alone, you are the most human people I know, the most reassuring in the world. If I call you monsters, then what name can I give to the so-called normal conditions that were foisted upon me? Look there, on the wall, the shadow of that frightful shoulder, the expression of that vast back and the neck swollen with blood . . . O monsters, do not leave me alone . . ."

They and I were confronted with identical dangers: an intractable man and a pernicious woman; we knew what it was to tremble with fright. At times I thought of them as less fortunate than I, because fright seized them unexpectedly, capriciously, according to the state of their nerves, whereas I always knew why my heart sank and why I trembled. But I envied them, since many of them were apt to confuse panic with the arousing of the senses. I envied them their chimera, close-shut in a cage and terrified. One of them, of whom I was very fond, kept his personal folly on a short and timid leash. He took it for a breath of its vital element in those parts of the city it and he knew, like the Chinese who go at evening to show their captive songbird the flowering gardens and the reflection of the setting sun among the reeds.

Pepe was—death now has him in safekeeping—a Spaniard of the old nobility, a small man, rather stiff and formal, chaste out of timidity, and agreeably ugly. He was hopelessly in love with blue and gold, pale gold, the blue and gold of the fair-haired working men in blue-denim overalls. Toward six o'clock in the evening, Pepe would lean against the balustrade of the Métro and watch, spellbound, all those shades of blue climb up from the dark underground, and the robust necks and the fair heads of hair. He tasted a pleasure that was purer than that tasted by the men who are attracted to working girls, for he neither made a move nor said a word. He had given me his friendship and unbosomed himself to me in his

French, which was correct but accented. No one has ever talked to me as he did of the colour blue or of golden hair curling like shavings around a reddened ear, or of the pungent populace of blond young working men.

"Pepe," I said, "write down what you have just told me!"

Modest Pepe, shocked to the depths of his lyrical feelings, lowered his eyes.

"That would not be at all amusing, my dear."

On fine warm evenings he took endless walks, searching, finding, and fleeing. The morose Paris of summertime became for Pepe an inferno, voluptuous and almost tropical. He described the wretched streets that I did not recognize, for under the vault of the twilight sky he set, like a tower of silver and gold, blue generator of light, some plumber's apprentice with Venetian blond hair, some metal worker spangled with copper. For a long time he loved those blond, blue-clad young males as one loves the immense sea, its every surge and swell. But one day the tide of six o'clock which empties the metallurgical and electrical workshops out onto the streets of Paris set before Pepe a nameless blue, blue of forget-me-not, of aconite, of gentian, of squill, with a golden pennon streaming across the face of . . .

"Oh!" stammered Pepe. "Vercingétorix!"

He pressed both hands against his heart that was at long last torn, and shut his lips. For a man has the right to murmur audibly "Adèle" or "Rose" and to kiss in public the portrait of a lady, but he must stifle the names of Daphnis or Ernest.

Pale, winged like those who go to their death, Pepe followed Vercingétorix. On the collar of the Gaul, in the folds of the elbow, and even on his boots, a fine fresh powder of metal sparkled, and sometimes his enormous moustache, obeying the evening breeze, almost whipped the back of his neck. He went into a nearby *tabac* so suddenly that he bumped into Pepe, who, stung by a point of the streaming moustache, staggered.

"*Pardon, monsieur,*" said Vercingétorix.

Dazed, Pepe told himself that he must be dreaming. "Or else I've just died," he thought. "The boy excused himself! He looked at me! He has just looked at me again . . . What's happened to my knees? My knees won't hold me up, but still I keep going, I'm following him, I . . ."

He stopped thinking, for Vercingétorix, turning around like an impudent street urchin, had smiled at him.

"I felt," Pepe related, "that shattering pang which warns us, deep in sleep, that a happy dream is ending. But I could not stop following him, and a half hour later I was climbing behind Vercingétorix a steep staircase and was sitting down in a small bedroom, very clean, very quiet, where there must have been net curtains, for everything seemed white. Vercingétorix had said, 'Sit down,' and had gone behind a ground-glass door. I believe I remained alone for quite a while. Such a thing had never happened to me before. I told myself, 'My heavens, he may kill me . . .' And I thought, 'Oh, if only he would kill me.' Because I realized that nothing better could happen. At last the door opened again and Vercingétorix . . ."

He clenched his boyish fists and banged them together.

"No, not Vercingétorix! No more Vercingétorix! Oh, what a horror he was! He had put on a woman's chemise laced with ribbons, cut low. And do you know what he had on his head? A . . . I almost don't dare to say it . . ."

He swallowed hard, made a face as if sickened.

"He had on his head a wreath of pompon roses. Pompon roses. With leaves. And with that soft pretty moustache below it . . . His beauty dishonoured! Oh, what a shameful masquerade . . ."

He fell into a bitter silence. I questioned him.

"But then what, Pepe? Afterward?"

"Afterward? Why, nothing," he said, astonished. "You perhaps don't find my story amusing enough. Afterward, I went away. I gave him something, left it on the table."

"Have you seen him again?"

"No, thank you very much," said Pepe, waving his hand. "I can see him well enough in my imagination . . . with the pompon roses. Never again in my life do I want to hear anyone talk about pompon roses . . ."

The fortune-tellers that he feverishly consulted—the woman in the rue Coulaincourt who fell into trances, the woman with the candle, the woman with the tarot cards, the woman with pins—kept predicting the same thing, and Pepe went from one to the other, leading a threatened life, for the pythonesses never stopped predicting that a big blonde woman was going to bring him to grief. They saw her quite easily through Pepe's small, slender body, which was attractive through some hard-to-define invalid's elegance, the hauteur of a hunchback without a hunch, the grace of the lame man without a short leg. When he finally had enough of giving the soothsayers the confused and travestied image of his infatuation, he disappeared, let himself be forgotten, then departed his uncomfortable life by an extremely tactful suicide, carefully prepared, colourless and well-bred, a suicide that disturbed no one.

# NINE

THEY HAVE SO PERFECTED their art of dissimulation that by comparison everything else seems imperfect. When I had to dissimulate, I had my models right there before my eyes. I had the daily example of a diplomacy laboriously practiced merely in the service of passion and resentment. I recall how a young man and his lover who were obliged to exercise great prudence were unmasked by a chatterbox and rather scandalously separated. The one most hurt of the two spent months on end trying to find a woman who would be attractive to the chatterbox's husband and succeeded all too terribly well.

Submerged in this project, he forgot himself, relegated his grief to a secondary place, studied and compared, arranged meetings, seized opportunities. Out of sheer exhaustion, he confided in me. Arriving with his harmless look of a young intellectual rather worn and haggard from his thankless work of translating, he would sink into a deep English armchair, green and hideous, lean back in it, and say, "I need to rest for a while." Which was a lie, for he shut his eyes out of circumspection, as a priest in the confessional shuts his eyes, separating himself from the penitent the better to see the form of the sin.

To dissimulate and keep up the dissimulation over a long period without ever flagging, through silences, through smiles, to appear to be an entirely different person—this relegates the trifling exaggerations of gossips to a quite inferior category. It is a task, as I've had occasion to notice since, which is only possible for the young; it is almost a kind of secretion, as native to young people as an insect's ability to elaborate its horny wing sheath, its casque and corselet of hard chitin... It would be a pity to let the memory of all this be lost. I keep it, as I keep, from these experiences, the ability to see beneath the surface and to outwit the admirable artifices of children and adolescents. Through this ability I enjoy better than many adults the forbidden pleasure of penetrating the world of the young, its brash lies, its elaborate and naïve constructions. Far from resenting my clairvoyance, my powerful yet puerile opponent with his multiplicity of faces enjoys the game, gives up when caught, and shows with a delighted blush the exact sensitive point I have struck.

Insight—the titillating knack for hurting! Reward granted for measuring, for intuiting the oscillations, the pendulum swings of "give and take"! A force that decreases does not go without appropriating to itself in passing some juxtaposing and consenting forces. "We come to you for warmth," declare my young friends of both sexes, wearing their youthful wounds like decorations, some of them still glistening with a trace of fresh blood, battered from recent blows. "Warm us, make us well!" they repeat. Many of them come to crouch down close to me and wait, resting a confused head against my knees

... O innocents! I tremble lest they be mistaken and, starting out as mendicants, may find they are the givers of life. Shall I ever know what I take from those who have trusted me? Did I owe them nothing more than to warm them? To receive from someone happiness—there's no avoiding using that word I do not comprehend—is it not to choose the sauce in which we want to be served up?

Scruples come to me, as usual, by extrahuman routes. The feeling has grown in me that I owe a debt to the animals which have dedicated their brief existence to me. Am I their guardian? My role is more nearly raptorial. Perhaps, after all, the true friend of animals is the one who groans in exasperation, "Oh, how that dog wears me out!" "Take away this cat, I can't think while he's in the room!" While I knowingly exhaust the dog, since he always yields, and usually when I say, "Come, puss," I see the cat hurry forward, even if reluctantly, and the cat is the abundant reservoir from which I draw secret clairvoyance, warmth, fantasy, self-control. Birds are too far removed from us, although the tufted titmouse shows a preference for me. But I remember that "catless" period of my life, which lasted about two years, was a time out of joint, a barren epoch. Whether one has to do with an animal or a child, to convince is to conquer and subdue. Just two hundred steps from this table lives a little four-year-old girl who fears neither spanking nor thunder and lightning nor wasps, and so assured is she of her power of seduction that she is practically uncontrollable. Sometimes, towards the end of the day, when her father is yawning with nervous exhaustion, when the violet shadows that ring the large eyes of her young mother make them seem larger, the child's nurse, white-faced, comes to fetch me: "*She* is terrible. *She* did not want to take her nap this afternoon. We are worn out, but *she* is as fresh as a daisy . . ."

Then I climb the neighbouring alleyway, and I confront the All-Powerful. Far from treating me as a scarecrow, the All-Powerful smiles at me, greets me, and starts a conversation on the exaggerated importance given to stewed peaches in her alimentation, for instance, or she criticizes my way of dressing: "You're not at all pretty in pyjamas, I like you better in a skirt," or she will show a great fondness for ancient French folk-lore and will sing an old ditty for me:

> *Early this morning*
> *Ragotin-dandy*
> *Drank so much brandy*
> *That he's staggering,*
> *Staggering!*

My role is to act indifferent and to read beneath the changing features of the All-Powerful her real thoughts. Shameful métier, in which I succeed all too well. Why is it that, without means other than my eyes and words, I

---

\* Ce matin,
Ragotin
A tant bu de brandevin
Qu'il branle!
Qu'il branle!

leave the All-Powerful mollified and overcome with sleep?
Seeing her so sensible and smiling with self-satisfaction,
I am reminded of a pair of little horses, glossy with indolence and oats, which, taken from the stable and harnessed, immediately broke the shafts and the traces. We
harnessed them again and they were soft as soap beneath
my hands, trotting sweetly when I took them again from
their master. "You have the hand of an old coachman, a
hand that puts a horse to sleep," he said, by way of prais-
ing me. For some human beings are utterly unacquainted
with a certain kind of piracy.

But my rival, the All-Powerful, will have her turn,
when I become enfeebled. Hovering over me like a
dragonfly, she will murmur, "There, there ... Rest, go
to sleep," and to my astonishment I shall sleep. We've not
reached that point, yet—oh, that involuntary start of
pride!—I am still strong enough to be lavish with my
gifts as well as to plunder the riches of others. If I had no
equals, I would tire of this twofold occupation, this acting
like a robber one minute and like a spendthrift the next.
But, apart from those individuals who hurriedly let themselves be filled by me, leaving me empty and drawn, and
apart from the superabundant ones, still worse, whose
indigestible contributions I quickly reject, there spreads a
zone where I can disport with my equals. I have more of
these than I could have expected. They are usually just
emerging from the worst kind of youth, the second childhood. They have lost their solemnity and have acquired
a sane notion of what is incurable and what is curable—
for instance, love. Ingeniously they fill each day from one

dawn to the next, and they have an adventurous spirit. They perceive, as I do, the pernicious element in daily work, and they do not laugh when I repeat the quip of a great journalist who died young and in harness: "Man is not made to work, and the proof is that work tires him." In short, they are frivolous, as have been hundreds of heroes. They have become frivolous the hard way. And they secrete from one day to the next their own ethics, which makes them even more understandable to me and colours them variously.

The thing we all have in common is a certain diffidence: we never dare to show openly that we need each other. Such reserve acts as a code of behaviour and constitutes what I call our "etiquette of survivors". Cast upon a rocky coast by their dismasted vessel, should not the survivors of the shipwreck be the most considerate of messmates? It is wise to apply the oil of refined politeness to the mechanism of friendship. Listen now to my friend, the painter-engraver D., and his Polynesian tactfulness. He had ceremoniously prepared his visit by a telephone call, and now he enters and noiselessly occupies the whole room, like a cloud.

"Madame Colette, I have come to excuse myself, I cannot dine with you tomorrow. I'm sorry, I'm really very upset, but since I've promised . . ."

He lowers his eyes in his reserved way, his wide shoulders fill the window, blocking the light as he stands there, dense and motionless as a wall. He speaks in an almost inaudible voice, without gestures, quite aware that a movement of his body, his suddenly raised voice could bring down the ceiling and shatter to bits my collection of milk glass.

"I would not have allowed myself to promise," D. goes on in a hurried whisper, "but it's a rather exceptional circumstance. I'm expecting a friend. We haven't seen each other in a long time, it will soon be five years, just imagine. I should explain that he has been absent . . . He's a lad who has had troubles, a great many troubles. He's returning from a distance and is going to feel very disoriented. The fact is, he was accused of having killed his grandmother and cut her up into pieces—what won't they think up next! Not only did they accuse him, they condemned him, like that, without proof. And worse still, they unearthed—the word is exact—an old yarn concerning a little girl who had been more or less raped . . . All this was quite badly demonstrated. In short, my friend has been away for five years. Just imagine how changed he will find things! So I promised to meet him at the station and to have dinner with him tomorrow. By jove, all those things that have been said about him . . ."

The rigidly extended arm of D., like a supporting beam, divides the room into two parts, on the one side "the things that have been said" and on the other side the sentimental truth.

". . . I simply disregard. But what I can assure you, Madame Colette, and I know him well, is that the boy is . . ."

A big hand, spread flat, marks and covers the location of an even greater heart, while his voice, muffled with tenderness, murmurs like the rustling of leaves:

[160]

". . . is infinitely gentle and refined. I might have asked your permission to bring him with me to dinner, but I felt I must refrain from making such a request . . ."

While speaking, the big man is tenderly handling a tiny frigate in spun glass; now he looks up at me, flashing me a facetious glance, his eyes as innocent as those of a young girl:

". . . because my friend is so shy . . ."

I allow this last word to keep all its naïve value. Not that, when listening to him, I am duped by so much artlessness—no more than D. himself is—or if so, just barely. That an assassin may be prudish or nervy, one can allow; it is by no means surprising. What I find significant when listening to D. is his respect for my personal conception of his character. An ideogram is comprised of heavy and light strokes, one must often press down hard when tracing a pattern, must use in a decorative way the dark stain in the background. Instinct and unbridled Herculean strength do not alone impel my friend D. to settle a public row by knocking two crazed heads together. Not in one day or spontaneously is a thoughtful "Polynesian" like D. fashioned, or a "child of nature" such as I. He and I and others like us come from the distant past and are inclined to cherish the arbitrary, to prefer passion to goodness, to prefer combat to discussion. Taken together and in good company, are these mental liberties enchanting? Certainly. Yes, yes. And without danger—without any other danger than not to have any more danger to run.

But scarcely have I praised these parallels and affinities when I cease to enjoy myself and begin to feel a malaise such as one experiences in the great museums among the crowded masterpieces, the painted faces, the portraits in which life continues to surge with baleful abundance.

Remove from me everything that is too sweet! Arrange for me, in the last third of my life, a clear space where I can put my favourite crudity, love. Merely to have it before me and to breathe it in, merely to touch it with hand or tooth, it keeps me young.

What then has changed between us, between love and me? Nothing, unless myself, or love. Everything that proceeds from love still wears its colour and spreads it over me. But this jealousy, for example, which blooms in its side like a dark carnation? Have I not too soon plucked it? Jealousy, debasing suspicions, inquisitions, reserved for the hours of night and nudity, the ritual ferocities, have I not too soon said goodbye to all those daily tonics? Jealousy leaves no time to be bored; does it even leave time to grow old? My grandmother, the mean one—that was the way I distinguished her from the other grandmother, who was apparently kind—at sixty years of age and more, followed my grandfather to the door of a certain *petit endroit*. When my mother was scandalized, the jealous old Provençal lady haughtily instructed her: "Eh, my girl, a man who wants to deceive us manages to escape through even smaller holes."

Her grey-green eyes were shaded by low reddish eyebrows, she moved with a dense corporeal majesty, in wide black taffeta skirts, and when so close to the end, she did not hesitate to treat love familiarly, with suspicion. I believe she was right to do so. It is right not to deny one's

[162]

self too soon all familiarity with the big impressive gestures which only jealousy can teach us, the big facile and murderous gestures, meticulously premeditated, so masterfully accomplished in imagination that it is foolish and pointless to carry them out.

The feminine faculty of anticipating or inventing what can and will happen is acute, and almost unknown to men. A woman knows all about a crime she may possibly commit. Maintained, if I may so express it, in a platonic state, amorous jealousy stimulates our gift of divination, strains all the senses, reinforces self-command. But what woman has not been disappointed in her crime, once she has committed it and the murdered lover lies there at her feet? "It was finer, the way I planned it. Is blood on the rug always dull and black like this? And that strange look of discontent, that disapproving sleep on a face, is it death, really death?"

She preferred her dreadful crime when she was carrying it within her, heavy and vibrant, finished in every detail and ready to break out into the world, like a child in the last hours of gestation. "But it didn't need to have all this reality ... Reality makes it seem so old, so commonplace and boring. But now here it is, the hour of my greatest torment, the hour when I organize each day a new setting for my great torment, for the ups and downs that I had not yet imagined, a catastrophe, a miracle. I did not want to exchange my great torment except for peace—if I have been mistaken, what will become of me?" She perceives that murder is always a fool's bargain. But she accepts it with difficulty, stubbornly she regards as an end what is only a beginning. Hence she must go on humiliating herself until she realizes there are only two kinds of human beings: those who have killed and those who have not killed.

I have had occasion to descend to the very depths of jealousy, have settled into it and thought about it at great length. It is not an unendurable sojourn, although in my writings in bygone days I believe I compared it, as everyone does, to a sojourn in hell, and I trust that the word will be put down to my poetic exaggeration. Rather, I would say, it is a kind of gymnast's purgatory, where the senses are trained, one by one, and it has the gloom of all training centres. Of course, I am talking about motivated, avowable jealousy, and not about an obsession. The sense of hearing becomes refined, one acquires visual virtuosity, a rapid and hushed step, a sense of smell that can capture the particles deposited in the atmosphere by a head of hair, a scented powder, the passage of a brazenly happy person —all this strongly recalls the field exercises of the soldier or the hypersensitive skill of poachers. A body absolutely on the alert becomes weightless, moves with somnambulistic ease, rarely collapses and falls. I would go so far as to affirm that it is so protected by its state of trance that it escapes the ordinary epidemics, provided, naturally, that one respects the rigid and special hygiene of the jealous person, eating enough and disdaining drugs. All the rest is, according to one's character, as boring as any solitary sport, as immoral as a game of chance. All the rest is a series of wagers lost or won, especially won. "What did I tell you? I told you He was meeting her every day at the same teashop. I was sure of it!" All the rest is competition: in beauty, in health, in obstinacy, in salacity, even. All the rest is hope . . .

Jealousy even thrives on homicidal desires. Inevitably. Checked, then released briefly like an elastic band, it almost has the virtues of an exercising apparatus. Leaving aside the hours darkened by sensual desires, when one is always ready to shout "Stop thief!" and to pose as being mistreated and starved for love, I deny that the pangs of jealousy keep us from living, working, even behaving like respectable people.

However, I see I have just employed, carelessly, the expression "to descend into the depths of jealousy". Jealousy is not at all low, but it catches us humbled and bowed down, at first sight. For it is the only suffering that we endure without ever becoming used to it. I am calling upon my memories here, my most faithful memories, that is to say, those that do not demand the help of superfluous accessories such as a night of wind, a mossy stone bench, the barking of a dog in the distance, arabesques of light and shadow on a wall or on a dress. Jealousy, by its tinctorial power, instills a strong and definitive colour to everything it encounters. If I wish, for example, to resuscitate a carnal moment—"thus I was caressed, thus I caressed, yes, thus, thus . . ."—an ironical mist hides and deforms what happened, what is no longer timely.

But let a certain phase of the moon take, at my order, its customary place in the sky, and simultaneously let a certain decaying elbow-rest at a window splinter beneath my fingernail, as it did thirty years ago, and the two compose an escutcheon of jealousy, and I see, on a field vert, the green of fine, stiff woodland grass piercing the dead leaves with its lances and brandishing them in the air. O flat Moon, round, then waning and less round, worm-eaten old wood, various other allegories, are you all that remains to me of a possession hotly and vainly disputed? No, I now have the ability to think about jealousy without experiencing burning transports, and can hear the echo of a name as if it were merely the distant and musical drone of an enormous swarm of bees. That is what constitutes one of the by no means negative recompenses, considerable, though vague, like one of those diplomas in which the whole place of honour on a parchment is filled with the word DIPLOMA. Who would think of trying to decipher the fine and complicated calligraphy below that word, faded and dim in the gloom of a parlour?

Like everyone, I have wanted death and a little more to claim a woman, two women, three women ... I am talking now about those acts of sympathetic magic which do not seriously harm anyone, not even the one who casts the spells, provided the people concerned are strong and hearty. They will get off with a confused and transient uneasiness, a feeling of languor, a few slight shocks such as might be caused by a finger laid on one's shoulder. But these are the messages that are sent by love as well as by hate, so I cannot guarantee their complete harmlessness.

During a rather burning season of jealousy, I myself

ran some risks. A rival of mine, very insecure in her happiness, thought of me strongly, and strongly I thought of her. But I made the mistake of letting myself go back to my writing, which demanded my attention, and to abandon my other task of antagonism, of daily and secret defiance. In short, I postponed my curses during three or four months, while Madame X continued hers, devoting her long hours of leisure to this. And I soon became aware of the results of such inequality. I began by falling into a ditch in the Place du Trocadéro, then I caught bronchitis. Then, in the Métro, on my way to the publisher, I lost the last part of a manuscript of which I had not kept a duplicate. A taxi driver short-changed me, leaving me on a rainy night without a sou. Then a mysterious epidemic bore off three of my Angora kittens...

To put an end to the series of misfortunes, I had only to arouse myself from an inexcusable negligence and to return once more to an even exchange of mental trajectories with Madame X. And we lived on mutually bad terms until the bond between us was worn out and space ceased to be a pathway of wicked beams of thought, a harp of resonant waves, a starry ether hung with signs and portents. I was not the only one to regret it, for we had quarrelled without feeling any fundamental antipathy. Time recompenses honourable adversaries. Mine, as soon as she stopped being an adversary, had some delightful anecdotes to tell which could amuse only ourselves.

"One day when I was going to Rambouillet to murder you..."

The rest of this story was a gay vaudeville, an involved

[167]

tale of a missed train, a stalled car, a gold-mesh handbag that burst open at the bottom, spilling out an indiscreet revolver upon the Rambouillet pavement, of inopportune encounters, of a friend who read in the periwinkle blue eyes of Madame X a homicidal intent and by some fond diplomacy diverted her from it . . .

"My dear," she exclaimed, "just count all these little happenings which raised chance obstructions between you and me in the town of Rambouillet! Can you deny that they were providential?"

"God forbid! There is one, especially, that I would hate to forget."

"Which one?"

"You see, I wasn't in Rambouillet at the time. I didn't set foot there that year."

"You weren't in Rambouillet?"

"I was not in Rambouillet."

"Well! That is the absolute limit!"

This limit revived, for some unknown reason, a little of the former resentment in the periwinkle eyes that questioned mine. But it was only a fleeting gleam. In vain we tried—in vain we still try—to upset each other by violent arguments, a tone of defiance quite out of keeping with our calm remarks: we soon recover our cordial relations. The powerful bond that was our youthful and mutual hatred can no longer unite us.

With that beautiful blue-eyed woman, whose light chestnut hair was exactly the shade of mine—and with such and such another and still another woman—I have ceased to exchange, shall never more exchange because of

[168]

a man and through a man that menacing thought, those reflections from mirror to mirror, that tireless emanation which wronged the lover himself ... "What are you thinking about?" he asked them. They were thinking about me. "But where are you, please?" he asked me when he saw I was not listening to him. "In the moon?" I was in spirit close to some woman, my invisible presence was upsetting her. We lacked nothing, those women and I: we had every kind of trouble.

Halfway between them and me, in an immunized zone, "He" lorded it, not as umpire but rather as the prize over which we fought. "They"—the men—are not fond of such subtle games and dread the fury of two females locked in combat. But a contest, even a terrible one, demands something more than passion. It demands sportsmanlike qualities and an equable temper even in the very midst of ferocious feelings. I do not have one jot of the sporting spirit, and therefore I indulged in fantasy, dealt blows below the belt that must be counted as foul or as failing to obey the rules of a game. I committed only one real fault, but I repeated it and was duly punished. Which was only just. An old saying warns us never to give either a boat or a bird. I would add: or a man. To begin with, because a man never—even when he swears it on our head or on the Holy Book—a man never belongs to us. And if by chance he lets himself be treated as our property, even gladly, he is so constituted that he would never forgive us for it. And since he rarely forgives the happy beneficiary, once again renouncement will have spoiled everything.

If you succeed, as I did, in sublimating the sexual drive and putting it in the service of heaven knows what mortifying joy or egalitarian madness, you will see the furious flower of jealousy stripped of its thorns, along with the condign egotism of the human couple.

What would a father confessor think of these agreed-to abdications, the handing-over of the rights of the bed? I am sure of his response, I who have never had an authorized confidant. He would think, as I do, that there is something about certain conjugal permissiveness that reminds one of the stuffiness of a closed room, and that the calm surface of these spurious families of doubtful respectability is worse than equivocal. Can one exist on lukewarmness? No better than one can live on vice—which, incidentally, stands to lose nothing in such conjugal arrangements.

What a lot of time wasted in absolutions! The most imbecile of all is that which literature has sanctified as "the eternal triangle". Its shocking variations, its acrobatic aspects of human pyramid very quickly discouraged the hesitating polygamous societies. What woman, no matter how foolish and unsettled, could be made to believe that one plus one equals three? Speaking as an onlooker, a cool-headed woman I know, unconventional but not without lucidity, assured me that in an eternal triangle there is always one person who is betrayed, and often two. I like to think that the one most constantly betrayed is the patriarch *in camera*, the clandestine Mormon. He well deserves it, in his traditional role of *agent provocateur*, and as a small-scale pasha.

His snare, a crude one, since it is nothing but sexual satisfaction, is set against him, if one of the two women he brings together improperly has some strength of character and withholds herself for the benefit of the weaker woman, withdrawing from the arrangement that has set them face to face, or, to put it more coarsely, mouth to mouth. The weak one normally yields, sheds her veil, demands a tender relationship with the other woman and gives her unquestioning devotion. "Trust me utterly, since I now have nothing to hide from you, I feel pure, I am your ally and no longer your victim."

Women pair off like this oftener than one might think. But having entered this state by a narrow tunnel, they prefer and are entitled to keep their union secret. Not long ago, one woman of such a pair died, and her friend quite literally sank into a decline. She did not make haste, she did not woo death, nor did she seek what she could never again possess, what she had never hoped for, what she explained so confusedly: "No, she was not like a daughter to me, for I doubt that genuine maternal feeling ever rids itself, even momentarily, of all hostile feeling. No, she was not like a lover to me, for I forgot that she was beautiful, that we had come together in despite of a man, in the deep and growing indifference we felt towards that man. We were joined in an infinity so pure that I never thought of death . . ."

As that word "pure" fell from her lips, I heard the trembling of the plaintive "u," the icy limpidity of the "r," and the sound aroused nothing in me but the need to hear again its unique resonance, its echo of a drop that

[171]

trickles out, breaks off, and falls somewhere with a plash. The word "pure" has never revealed an intelligible meaning to me. I can only use the word to quench an optical thirst for purity in the transparencies that evoke it —in bubbles, in a volume of water, and in the imaginary latitudes entrenched, beyond reach, at the very centre of a dense crystal.